Benjamin Leopold Farjeon

Basil and Annette

Vol. II

Benjamin Leopold Farjeon

Basil and Annette
Vol. II

ISBN/EAN: 9783337066444

Printed in Europe, USA, Canada, Australia, Japan

Cover: Foto ©Andreas Hilbeck / pixelio.de

More available books at **www.hansebooks.com**

BASIL AND ANNETTE.

BASIL AND ANNETTE.

A Novel.

BY

B. L. FARJEON.

AUTHOR OF

"BLADE-O'-GRASS," "GRIF," "TOILERS OF BABYLON,"
"THE MYSTERY OF M. FELIX," ETC.

IN THREE VOLUMES.

VOL. II.

LONDON:
F. V. WHITE & CO.,
31, SOUTHAMPTON STREET, STRAND, W.C.
1890.

PRINTED BY
KELLY AND CO., GATE STREET, LINCOLN'S INN FIELDS,
AND KINGSTON-ON-THAMES.

CONTENTS.

— ◆ -

BASIL AND ANNETTE.

BASIL AND ANNETTE.

CHAPTER I.

A MALICIOUS smile played about the old man's lips as he glanced at Basil and Annette. For a few moments he did not speak, but stood enjoying the situation, feeling himself master of it ; and when he broke the silence his voice was smooth and suave. The malignancy of his feelings was to be found in his words, not in the tone in which he uttered them.

" Ah, Mr. Basil Whittingham once more ; Mr. Basil Whittingham, the English gentleman, ready at a moment's notice to give lessons in manners, conduct, and good breeding. But then it is to proclaim oneself a fool to take a man at his own estimate of himself. I find you here in the company of my niece. Favour me with an explanation, Mr. Basil Whittingham."

"There is nothing to explain," said Basil, still with his arm round Annette. "I have been absent some time, and happening, fortunately, to return before Miss Bidaud left the country have met her here, and was exchanging a few words of farewell."

"Of course, of course. Who would venture to dispute with so reproachless a gentleman? Who would venture to whisper that in these last few words of farewell there was any attempt to work upon a child's feelings, and to make the spurious metal of self-interest shine like purest gold? On one side a young girl, as yet a mere child, whose feelings are easily worked upon; on the other side a grown man versed in the cunning of the world, and using it with a keen eye to profitable use in the future. Not quite an equal match, it appears to me, but I may be no judge. If I were to hint that this meeting between you and my dear niece and ward has anything of a clandestine nature in it, you would probably treat me to a display of indignant fireworks. If I were to hint that, instead of so advising this child that she should hold out her arms gladly to the new life into which she is about to enter, you were instilling into her a feeling of repugnance against it, and of mistrust against those whose duty it will be to guide her aright and teach her—principles "—his eyes twinkled with malignant humour as he spoke this word—" you, English gentleman that you are, would repudiate the insinuation with lofty scorn. But when you exchange confidences with me you are in the presence of a man who has also seen something of the world, and who, although it has dealt him hard buffets, retains some old-fashioned notions of honour and manliness. I apply the test to you, adventurer, and you become instantly exposed. Ah! here is my sister, this sweet young child's aunt, who will relieve you of your burden."

He took the hand of the unresisting girl and led her to her aunt, whose arm glided round Annette's waist, holding it as in a vice.

"I will not answer you," said Basil, with an encouraging smile at Annette, whose face instantly brightened. "Annette knows I have spoken the truth, and that is enough."

"Yes, Basil," said Annette, boldly, "you have spoken the truth, and I will never, never forget what you have said to me to-day."

"Take her away," said Gilbert Bidaud to his sister; "the farce is played out. In a week it will be forgotten."

"Good-bye, Basil," said Annette, "and God bless you."

"Good-bye, Annette," said Basil, "and God guard you."

"How touching, how touching!" murmured Gilbert Bidaud. "It is surely a scene from an old comedy. Take her away."

"Just one moment, please," said old Corrie, joining the group. "Here is something that belongs to the little lady, that she would like to take with her to the new world. It will remind her of the old, and of friends she leaves in it."

It was the magpie in its wicker cage, whose tongue being loosened by company, or perhaps by a desire to show off its accomplishments to an appreciative audience, became volubly communicative.

"Basil! Basil! Basil and Annette! Little lady! Little lady!"

In his heart Gilbert Bidaud was disposed to strangle the bird, but his smile was amiability itself as he said to Annette, "Yours, my child?"

" Yes, mine," she answered. " Mr. Corrie gave it to me."

" But Mr. Corrie is not rich," said Gilbert Bidaud, pulling out his purse; " you are. Shall we not pay him for it? "

" No," said Annette, before old Corrie could speak. " I would not care for it if he took money for it."

" Well said, little lady," said old Corrie; " the bird is friendship's offering, and for that will be valued and well cared for, I don't doubt. It is your property, mind, and no one has a right to meddle with it."

" Friendship's offering! " said Gilbert Bidaud, with a long, quiet laugh. " We came out to the bush to learn something, did we not, sister? Why, here we find the finest of human virtues and sentiments, the smuggest of moralities, the essence of refined feeling. It is really refreshing. Do not be afraid, Mr. Corrie. Although I would not take your word about that wood-splitting contract, I have some respect for you, as a rough specimen of bush life and manners. We part friends, I hope."

" Not a bit of it," said old Corrie. " If ladies were not present I'd open my mind to you."

"Thank heaven," said Gilbert Bidaud, raising his eyes with mock devotion, "for the restraining influence of the gentler sex. You do not diminish my esteem for you. I know rough honesty when I meet with it."

"You shift about," interrupted old Corrie, "like a treacherous wind. I'm rough honesty now, am I? You're the kind of man that can turn white into black. Let us make things equal by another sort of bargain. I've given little lady the bird. You'll not take it from her?"

"Heavens?" cried Gilbert Bidaud, clasping his hands. "What do you think of me?"

"That's not an answer. You'll not take it from her?"

"I will not. Keep it, my child, and be happy."

"Do you hear, little lady? Let us be thankful for small mercies. Shake hands, my dear. When you're a woman grown, don't forget old Corrie."

"I never will—I never will," sobbed Annette.

"And don't forget," said old Corrie, laying his hand on Basil's shoulder, "that Master Basil here is a gentleman to be honoured and loved, a man to be proud of, a man to treasure in your heart."

"I will never forget it," said Annette, with a fond look at Basil.

"And this, I think," said Gilbert Bidaud, with genial smiles all round, "is the end of an act. Let the curtain fall to slow music."

But it was not destined so to fall. As Annette's aunt turned to leave with her niece, her eyes, dwelling scornfully on Basil for a moment, caught sight of the chain attached to the locket which Annette had put round his neck. Quick as lightning she put her hand to the child's neck, and discovered the loss.

"He has stolen Annette's locket!" she cried, pointing to the chain.

As quick in his movements as his sister, Gilbert Bidaud stretched forth his hand and tore the locket and chain from Basil's neck. It was done so swiftly and suddenly that Basil was unable to prevent it; but the hot blood rushed into his face as he said:

"Were you a younger man I would give you cause to remember your violence. Annette, speak the truth."

"I gave it to you, Basil," said Annette,

slipping from her aunt's grasp, and putting
her hand on Gilbert Bidaud's. " It is false
to say he stole it. It belonged to me, and I
could do what I pleased with it. I gave it to
Basil, and he did not want to take it at first,
but I made him."

She strove to wrench it from her uncle's
hand, but it was easy for him to keep it from
her.

" I will have it !" cried Annette. " I will,
I will! It is Basil's, and you have no right
to it."

" A storm in a teapot," said Gilbert Bidaud,
who seldom lost his self-possession for longer
than a moment. " Sister, you should apolo-
gise to the young gentleman. Take the
precious gift."

But instead of handing it to Basil he threw
it over the young man's head, and Newman
Chaytor, who during the whole of this scene
had been skulking, unseen, in the rear, and
had heard every word of the conversation,
caught it before it fell, and slunk off with it.

" I shall find it, Annette," said Basil.
" Good-bye, once more. May your life be
bright and happy !"

Those were the last words, and being

uttered at the moment Newman Chaytor caught the locket and was slinking off, were heard and treasured by him.

The whole of that day Basil, assisted by old Corrie and Chaytor, searched for the locket, of course unsuccessfully. He was in great distress at the loss; it seemed to be ominous of misfortune.

CHAPTER II.

THE story of the lives of Basil and Chaytor during the ensuing three years may be briefly summarised. So far as obtaining more than sufficient gold for the bare necessaries of life was concerned, ill-luck pursued them. They went from goldfield to goldfield, and followed every new rush they heard of, and were never successful in striking a rich claim. It was all the more tantalising because they were within a few feet of great fortune at least half-a-dozen times. On one gold-field they marked out ground, close to a claim of fabulous richness, every bucket of wash-dirt that was hauled from the gutter being heavily weighted with gold. This was the prospectors' claim, and the shaft next to it struck the gutter to the tune of twelve ounces a day per man. The same with the second, and Basil and Chaytor had every reason, therefore, to congratulate themselves, especially when the men working in the claim beyond them also struck the lead, and struck it rich. But when at length the two gold diggers in whom we are chiefly interested came upon the gutter, they were dismayed to find that instead of ten ounces to the tub, it was as much as they could do to wash out ten grains. It was the only poor claim along the whole of the gutter ; on each side of them the diggers were coining money, and they were literally beggars. It is frequently so on the goldfields, the life on which very much resembles a lottery, riches next door to poverty ; but the hope of turning up a lucky number seldom dies out in the heart of the miner. He growls a bit, apostrophises his hard luck in strong language, is despondent for a day, and the next shakes off his despondent fit, and buckles to again with a will, going perhaps to another new rush, jubilant and full of hope, to meet again with the same bad fortune. The romance of the goldfield is a rich vein for novelists, some few of whom have tapped it successfully ; but the theme is far from being worn out, and presents as tempting material to-day as it did years ago, when gold was first discovered in Australia.

" It is maddening, Basil," said Chaytor, as

he gazed gloomily at the " prospect " in his
tin dish, two or three specks which would not
have covered a pin's head. " Here we are
upon the gutter again, and the stuff will wash
about half a pennyweight to the tub."

" It's jolly hard," said Basil, proceeding to
fill his pipe with cut cavendish, " but what can
we do? Grin and bear it."

" Ah, you're philosophical, you are," growled
Chaytor, " but I'm not so easy minded. Just
think of it, and bring a little spirit to bear
upon it, will you? "

" Off you go," said Basil. " I'm listening."

" Here we are on Dead Man's Flat, and here
we've been these last three weeks. Just four
days and three weeks ago we struck our claim
in Mountain Maid Gully, having got two
ounces and three pennyweights for our month's
hard work. That contemptible parcel of gold
brought us in barely eight pounds, the gold
buyer pretending to blow away sand before he
put it in the scale, but blowing away more
than two pennyweights of the stuff, and reduc-
ing it to a little over two ounces. We weighed
it in our own gold scales before we took it to
him, and it was two ounces three pennyweights
full weight. You can't deny that."

"I've no intention of denying it. Don't be irritable. Go on, and let off steam; it will do you good."

"I want to point out this thing particularly," fumed Chaytor, "so that we can get to the rights of our ill luck, get to the bottom of it, I mean, and find out the why and the wherefore. Eight pounds we receive for our gold, when we should have received eight pounds ten; not a sixpence less; but the world is full of thieves. Now, that eight pounds gives us a little under twenty shillings a week a man. I would sooner starve."

"I wouldn't—though I've had bitter blows, Chaytor."

"Not worse than I have."

"It is the pinching of our own shoes we feel, old fellow. We're a selfish lot of brutes. Thank you for pulling me up. I'm sorry for you, Chaytor."

"And I'm sorry for you. Thinking our claim worthless we leave Mountain Maid Gully, and come here to Dead Man's Flat. We are ready to jump out of our skins with joy, for we come just in time—so we think. Here's a new lead struck, with big nuggets in it, and we mark out our claim exactly one

hundred and twenty feet from the prospectors'
ground. They get one day twenty ounces,
the next day twenty-eight, the next day forty-
two—a fortune, if it lasts."

" Which it seldom does."

" It often does, and even if it lasts only six
or seven weeks it brings in a lot. ' We're in
luck this time,' I say to you, and I dream of
nuggets as big as my head. The gutter, we
reckon, is forty feet down, and we reach it in
three weeks. Everybody round us is making
his pile—why shouldn't we ? But before we
strike the lead a digger comes up, and says,
' Hallo, mates, have you heard about the claim
you left in Mountain Maid Gully ? ' ' No,' say
we, ' what about it ? '—' Oh,' says the digger,
' only that two new chums jumped into it after
you'd gone away and found out it was the
richest claim on the goldfield. They took a
thousand ounces out of it the second week
they were at work.' What do you say to that,
Basil ? "

" Jolly hard luck, Chaytor."

" Cursed hard luck, I say."

" Strong words won't better it."

" They're a relief. You take it philosophi-
cally, I admit ; I growl over it like a bear

with a sore head. I'd like to know why there's
this difference between us."

"I'll try and tell you presently, when
you've finished about the two claims."

"All right. I shouldn't be much of a man
if the news about the ground we ran away
from didn't rile me. I was so wild I could
hardly sleep that night. But when I heard
that in the next claim to the one we're working now a nugget weighing a hundred and
fifty ounces was found I thought perhaps we'd
got a richer claim than the one we'd deserted.
So I bottled up my bad temper, and went on
working with a good grace. And now we're
on the gutter again, and here's the result."
He held out the tin dish, and gazed at the tiny
specks of gold with disgust. "Why it's the
very worst we've struck yet."

"Not quite that. We've had as bad. What
shall we do? Stick to it, or try somewhere
else?"

"We daren't go away. Stick to it we must.
If we left it and I heard afterwards the same
sort of story we were told about our claim on
Mountain Maid, I should do somebody a mischief. You agree with me, then, that we
remain and work the claim out?"

" I agree to anything you wish, Chaytor. I
will stay or go away, just as you decide."

Chaytor looked at him with an eye of
curiosity. " Were you ever a fellow of
much strength of character, Basil ? "

" I think so, once ; not in any remarkable
degree, but sufficient for most purposes."

" And now ? "

" And now," replied Basil, taking his pipe
from his mouth, and holding it listlessly
between his fingers, " the life seems to have
gone out of me. The only tie that binds me
to it is you. I owe you an everlasting debt
of gratitude, old fellow, and I wish I could do
something to repay it. But in tying yourself
to me you are tied to a log that keeps dragging you down. The ill luck that pursues us
comes from me. Throw me off and fortune
will smile upon you."

" And upon you ? "

" No. The taste of all that's sweet and
beautiful has gone out of my mouth ; I'm a
soured man inside of me ; you're a thousand
times better than I am. What is bitterness in
you comes uppermost ; it pleases you to hide
the best part of you ; but you cannot hide it
from me, for I've had experience of you and

know you. Now I'm the exact reverse. Out-
wardly you would think I'm an easy-going,
easy-natured fellow, willing always to make
the best of things, and to look on the brightest
side. It is untrue; I am a living hypocrite.
Inwardly I revile the world; because of my
own disappointments I can see no good in it.
Good fortune or bad fortune, what does it
matter to me now? It cannot restore my
faith, it cannot destroy the shroud which
hangs over my heart. That is the difference
between us. You are a thoroughly good
fellow, I am a thoroughly bad one."   •

"It was not always the same with you.
How have you become soured?"

"Through experience. Look here, Chaytor,
it is only right you should be able to read me.
You have bared your heart to me, and it is
unfair that I should keep mine closed. There
have been times when business of your own
has called you to Sydney. We were never
rich enough to go together, so you had to go
alone, while I remained, in order not to lose
the particular luckless claim we happened to
be working in, and out of which we were
always going to make our fortune. On the
occasions of your visits you have executed a

small commission for me, entailing but little
trouble, but upon the successful result of
which I set great store. It was merely to
call at the Post-office, and ask for letters for
Basil Whittingham. The answer was always
the same : there were none. Every time you
returned and said, 'No letters for you, Basil,'
I suffered more than I can express. There
was less light in the world, my heart grew
old. I believe I did not betray myself; at all
events, I took pains not to do so."

"I never knew till now, Basil," said
Chaytor falsely, and in a tone of false pity,
"that you thought anything at all of not
receiving letters. You certainly succeeded in
making me believe that it did not matter one
way or another."

"That is what I have grown into, a living
hypocrite, as I have said. Why should I
inflict my troubles upon you? You have
enough of your own, and I have never been
free from the reproach that evil fortune
attends you because you persist in remaining
attached to me. But the honest truth is, I
suffered much, and each time the answer was
given there was an added pang to make my
sufferings greater. I'll tell you how it is with

me, or rather how it was, for were you torn
from me, were I pursuing my road of life
alone, I should feel like a ghost walking
through the world, cut off from love, cut off
from sympathy. Not so many years ago—
and yet it seems a lifetime—it was very different. I know I loved my dear mother, and
perhaps in a lesser degree, but still with a
full-hearted love, I loved my father. You
know the whole story of my life; I cannot
recall an incident of any importance in my
career in the old country and in others
through which I travelled which I have
omitted to tell you. Partly it was because
you took so deep an interest in me, partly
because it gratified me to dwell upon matters
which gave me pleasure. Yes, although my
shot was pretty well expended when I left
England for Australia, there is nothing in my
history there which causes me regret. Until
the death of my father everything looked fair
for me. It was a good world, a bright
world, with joyous possibilities in it, some of
which might in the future be realised. I spent
my fortune in paying my father's debts, and
though it alienated my uncle from me and
ruined my prospects, never for one moment

did I regret it. There was no merit due to me in doing what I did ; any man of right feeling would have done the same ; you would have been one of the first to do it. Well, I came out to the Colonies with a light heart and nearly empty pockets. I had my hardships—what mattered ? I was young, I was strong, I was hopeful, I believed in human goodness. So I went on my way till I came to Anthony Bidaud's plantation. There the sun burst forth in its most brilliant colours, and all my petty trials melted away. Had my nature been soured it would have been the same, I think, for love is like the sun shining upon ice. I met a man and a friend in Anthony Bidaud; we understood and esteemed each other. I met a little maid to whom my heart went out—you know whom I mean, little Annette. You never saw her, Chaytor. When she came to old Corrie's hut on the day we left Gum Flat, after you snatched me from a cruel death and nursed me to strength, you were wandering in the woods, and did not join us till she had gone. If you had met her you might have some idea of the feelings I entertained towards her, for although she was but a child

at the time, there was a peculiar attraction
and sweetness about her which could not
have failed to make an impression upon you.
You are acquainted with all that passed between me and Annette's father, of the project
he entertained of making me guardian to his
little daughter, and of his strange and sudden
death ; and you are also acquainted with the
unexpected appearance of Gilbert Bidaud
upon the scene, and what afterwards trans-
pired, to the day upon which he and his sister
and Annette left the colony for Europe. The
little maid promised faithfully to write to me
from Europe, and I gave her instructions,
which she could scarcely have forgotten, how
to communicate with me. Her letters were
to be directed to the Sydney Post-office, and
she was to let me know how to communicate
with her. Well, unreasonably or not, I fed
upon the expectation of these promised letters,
but they never came. We must have some
link of affection to hold on to in this world if
life is worth living, and this was the link to
which I clung. From old associations in
England I was absolutely cut away, not one
friend was left to me ; and when I arrived at
Anthony Bidaud's plantation and made An-

nette my friend, I felt as if all the sweetness
of life dwelt in her person. It was an ex-
aggerated view perhaps, but so it was. Since
that time three years have passed, and she is
as one dead to me, and I suppose I am as one
dead to her. For some little while after she
left I used to indulge in hopes of wealth, in
hopes of striking a golden claim and becoming
rich. Then I used to say to myself, I will go
home and wait till Annette is a woman, when
I will take her from the hateful influence of
Gilbert Bidaud, and—and—but, upon my
honour, my thoughts got no farther than this ;
my dreams and hopes were unformed beyond
the point of proving myself her truest and
best friend. But her silence has changed my
nature, and I no longer indulge in hopes and
dreams, I no longer desire riches. The
future is a blank : there is no brightness in it.
If it happens that we are fortunate, that after
all our ill luck we should strike a rich claim,
I will give you my share of the gold freely,
for I should have no use for it."

"I would not accept it, Basil," said
Chaytor; "we will share and share alike.
Have you no desire, then, to return to
England ? "

"I shall never go back," replied Basil. "My days will be ended in Australia."

"Where you will one day meet with a woman who will drive all thoughts of Annette out of your head."

"That can never be."

"You think of her still, then?"

"As she was, not as she is. I live upon the spirit of the past."

He spoke not as a young man, but as one who had lived long years of sad and bitter experience. In this he was unconsciously doing himself a great wrong, for his heart was as tender as ever, and in reality he had intense faith in the goodness of human nature; but the theme upon which he had been dilating always, when he reflected upon or spoke of it, filled his soul with gloom, and so completely dominated him with its melancholy as to make him unintentionally false to his true self.

"The question is," said Chaytor, "whether it is worth while to brood upon such a little matter. The heart of a child—what is it? A pulse with about as much meaning in it as the heart of an animal. There is no sincerity in it. I have no doubt you would be amazed if you were to know Annette as she is now, almost a woman, moulded after her uncle's teaching, and therefore repulsive in nature as he was. You are wise in your resolve to make no attempt to shatter an ideal. I have suffered myself in love and friendship, and I know better than you how little dependence is to be placed in woman. Let us get back to the claim. We'll not give it up till we've proved it quite worthless."

CHAPTER III.

HAD Basil been acquainted with the extent of Newman Chaytor's baseness and villainy he would have been confounded by the revelation. But unhappily for himself he was in entire ignorance of it, and it was out of the chivalry of his nature that he placed Chaytor on an eminence, in the way of human goodness, to which few persons can lay claim. But Basil was a man who formed ideals; it was a necessity of his existence, and it is such men who in their course through life are the most deeply wounded.

Chaytor's visits to Sydney were not upon business of his own, he had none to take him there; they were simply and solely made for the purpose of obtaining the letters which arrived for Basil from England, and any also which might arrive for himself; but these latter were of secondary importance. In his inquiries at the Post-office he was always

furnished with an order signed, "Basil Whittingham" (of which he was the forger) to
deliver to bearer any letters in that name.
Thus he was armed to meet a possible difficulty, although it would have been easy
enough to obtain Basil's letters without such
order. But as he had frequently observed
he was a man who never threw away a
chance.

As a matter of fact, he received letters
both for himself and Basil, which he kept
carefully concealed in an inner pocket. He
had become a man of method in the crooked
paths he was pursuing, and these letters,
before being packed away, were placed in a
wrapper, securely sealed, with written direc-
tions outside to the effect that if anything
happened to him and they fell into the hands
of another person they should be immediately
burnt. This insured their destruction in the
event of their falling into the hands of Basil,
for Chaytor had implicit faith in his comrade's quixotism and chivalry, at which he
laughed in his sleeve.

It has already been stated that Chaytor
had made himself a master of the peculiari-
ties of Basil's handwriting. Having served

his apprenticeship in his disgraceful career
in England he could now produce an imita-
tion of Basil's hand so perfect as to deceive
the most skilful of experts, who often in
genuine writing make mistakes which should,
but do not, confound them. Shortly after
Annette and her uncle and aunt had taken
their departure from Australia he wrote to
Basil's uncle in England. It is not necessary
to reproduce the letter ; sufficient to say that
it was chatty and agreeable, that it recalled
reminiscences which could not but be pleasant
to the old gentleman, that it abounded in
affectionate allusions, and wound up with the
expression of a hope that Mr. Bartholomew
Whittingham would live till he was a hundred in health and happiness. There was
not a word in the letter which could be con-
strued into the begging of a favour ; it was
all gratitude and affection ; and the writer
asked whether there was any special thing in
Australia which Mr. Bartholomew Whittingham would like to have. "Nothing would
give me greater pleasure," said the wily correspondent, "than to obtain and send it to
you in memory of dear old times. I will
hunt the emu for you ; I will even send you

home a kangaroo. God bless you, my dear
uncle! I have been a foolish fellow I know,
but what is done cannot be undone, and I
have only myself to blame. There, I did
not intend to make the most distant allusion
to anything in the past that has offended you,
but it slipped out, and I can only ask your
forgiveness." In a postscript the writer said
that his address was the Post Office, Sydney,
not, he observed, that he expected Mr.
Bartholomew Whittingham to write to him
or answer his letter, but there was no harm
in mentioning it. It was just such a letter as
would delight an old gentleman who had in
his heart of hearts a warm regard for the
young fellow whose conduct had displeased
him. Chaytor had some real ability in him,
which, developed in a straight way, would
have met with its reward ; but there are men
who cannot walk the straight paths, and
Chaytor was one of these.

Two months afterwards, before any answer
could have reached him, Chaytor wrote a
second letter, as bright and chatty as the
first, brimful of anecdote and story, and this
he despatched, curious as to the result of his
arrows. They hit the mark right in the

bull's-eye, but Chaytor was not quite aware
of this. However, he was satisfied some time
afterwards at receiving a brief note from a
firm of lawyers—not from Messrs. Rivington,
Sons, and Rivington, to whom he had been
articled, but from another firm, and for this
he was thankful—which said that Mr.
Bartholomew Whittingham had received his
nephew's letter, and was glad to learn that he
was in good health and spirits. That was all,
but it was enough for Chaytor. In the first
place it proved that his handwriting was
perfect and the circumstances he spoke of
correct. In the second place it proved that
Basil's uncle had a soft spot left for him and
that the writer had touched it. In the third
place it proved that his letters were welcome,
and that others would be acceptable.

"A good commencement," thought Chaytor. "I have but to play my cards boldly,
and the old fool's forty thousand pounds will
be mine. What a slice of luck for me that
Rivington, Sons, and Rivington no longer
transact his business! At a distance I could
deceive them. At close quarters their suspicions might be excited, although I would
chance even that, if there were no other way.

I wonder how long the old miser will live.
I am not anxious that he should die yet;
things are not ripe; there is Basil to get rid
of." He was ready and resolved for any
desperate expedient to compass his ends, and
he kept not only the letters he received, but
copies of the letters he sent, for future guid-
ance, if needed. Be sure that he continued
to write, and that he made not the slightest
reference to any hope of becoming the old
gentleman's heir, or of being reinstated in his
affections. It is strange how a man's intellect
and intelligence are sharpened when he is
following a congenial occupation. Machia-
velli himself could not have excelled Newman
Chaytor in the execution of the villainous
scheme he was bent upon carrying out. He
became even a fine judge of character, and
not a word he wrote was malapropos. Let
it be stated that, despite the risk he was
running, he derived genuine pleasure from
the plot he had devised. He thought himself,
with justice, a very clever fellow; if all went
on in England as he hoped it would he had
no fear as to being able to silence or get rid
of Basil on the Australian side of the world.
He would be a dolt indeed if he could not

remove a man so weak and trustful as Basil from his path. He had other letters from Mr. Bartholomew Whittingham's lawyers, and he knew, from a growing cordiality in their tone (a sentiment in which lawyers never of their own prompting indulge in their business transactions) that they were dictated by the old gentleman himself. His interpretation of Basil's uncle not writing in his own person was that he had made up his mind not to have any direct personal communication with his nephew, and that being of an obstinate disposition, he was not going to break his resolution. "For all that," thought Chaytor, "I will have his money. I'll take an even bet that he has either not destroyed his old will, or that he has made a new one, making Basil his heir. Newman Chaytor, there are not many who can beat you."

He received other letters as well from other persons—from his old mother, addressed to himself, and from Annette, addressed to Basil. Certainly when he went to Sydney his hands were full, and he had enough to do. He did not grudge the labour. He saw in the distance the pleasures of life awaiting him, and it is a fact that in time he came to believe that they were his to enjoy and that Basil had no rightful claim to them. It was he, Newman Chaytor, who had schemed for them, who was working for them. What was Basil doing? Nothing. Standing idly by, without making an effort to come into his own. "This is the way men get on," said Chaytor to himself, surveying with pride the letter he had just finished to Basil's uncle, "and I mean to get on. Why, the trouble of writing this letter alone is worth a thousand pounds. And what is the risk worth, I should like to know? I am earning double the money I shall get."

The letters of his old mother to himself were less frequent—not more than one every nine or ten months. They always commenced, "My dearly beloved son," and they plunged at once into a description of the difficulties with which she and her poor husband were battling. Her first letter gave him a piece of news which caused him great joy. It informed him that a certain bill which Chaytor had left behind him, dishonoured, had been bought by his father, at the sacrifice of some of the doubtful securities which he had saved from the wreck of his fortune. "You can come home with safety now, my dear son," wrote the unhappy old woman. "Well, that is a good hearing," mused Newman Chaytor; "I was always afraid of that bill; it might have turned up against me at any moment, but now it is disposed of, and I am safe. So, the old man still had something left worth money all the time he was preaching poverty to me. Such duplicity is disgusting. He owes me a lot for frightening me out of the country as he did. And here is the old woman going on with the preaching about hard times and poverty. Such selfishness is wicked, upon my soul it is." It was true that his mother's letters ran principally on the same theme. They had not a penny; they lived in one room; their rent was behindhand; her husband was more feeble than ever; they often went without food, for both she and he were determined to starve rather than appeal to the parish. Could not her dear son send them a trifle, if it was only a few shillings, to help them fight the battle which was drawing to its close? She hoped he would forgive her for asking him, but times were so hard, and the winter

was very severe. They had had no fire for
two days, and the landlady said if they could
not pay the last two weeks' rent that they
would have to turn out. "Try, my dear
boy, try, for the sake of the mother who bore
you, and who would sell her heart's blood for
you, if there was a market for it."

These letters annoyed Chaytor, and he
thought it horribly hard that his mother
should write them. "It is a try on," he
thought; "the old man has put her up to it.
I ought to know the ins and outs of such
transparent tricks. 'Now, write this,' says
the old man; 'Now write that. We must
manage to screw something out of him: work
upon his feelings, mother.' That's the way it
goes. I'll bet anything they've got a smoking
dinner on the table all the time, but Newman's
at a distance, and can't see it. Oh, no, I
can't see anything; a baby might impose
upon me." He never thought of the night he
saw his mother begging in the roadway with
a box of matches in her hands. Some men
are gifted with the power of shutting out
inconvenient memories, as there are others
who never lose sight of a kindness they have
received or of a debt that is justly due. Long

before this the reader has discovered to which class Chaytor belonged.

Nevertheless he replied to the letters, cantingly regretting that he was unable to send his dear old mother the smallest remittance to help her on in her struggles. "How is it possible," he wrote, "when I am myself starving? It is months since I have had a full meal, and I have had to work sixteen hours a day breaking stones on the road for a piece of dry bread. The hardships I have endured, and am still enduring, are frightful. This is a horrible place for a gentleman to live in. I should not have been here•if father had not driven me away. It almost drives me mad to think that if he had not been so hard to me, if he had allowed me to stop at home and manage his affairs, I could have pulled them straight, and that we should all of us be living now in comfort and plenty in the only country in the world where a man can enjoy his days. You have no idea what kind of place this colony is. Men die like lambs in the snow, and the sufferings they endure are shocking to contemplate. I do not suppose I shall live to write you another letter, but if you can manage to send me a

19*

few pounds it may arrive just in time to
save me." And so on, and so on. He took
a keen delight in the duplicities he was
practising, and he would read his letters
over with a feeling of pride and exultation in
his cleverness. "How many men are there
in the world," he would ask himself, "who
could write such a letter as this? Not many.
Upon my word I'm wasted in this hole and
corner. But there's by-and-by to come ;
when I get hold of that forty thousand
pounds I'll have my revenge. No galley
slave ever worked harder than I am working
for a future I mean to enjoy." That may
have been true enough, but the work of a
galley slave was honest labour in comparison
with that to which Newman Chaytor was
bending all his energies.

Lastly, there were the letters Annette
wrote to Basil. They arrived at intervals of
about four months, so that Chaytor was
in possession of seven or eight of them.
Proceeding as they did from a pure and
beautiful nature, these letters, had Basil
received them, would have been like wine to
him, would have comforted and strengthened
him through the hardest misfortunes and

troubles, would have kept the sun shining upon him in the midst of the bitterest storms. He would have continued to work with gladness and hope instead of with indifference. It would have made the future a bright goal to which his eyes would ever have been turned with joy. Evidences of kindness and sympathy, still more, evidences of unselfish affection and love, are like the dew to the flower. They keep the heart fresh, they keep its windows ever open to the light. But of this blessing Basil was robbed by the machinations of a scoundrel: hence there was no sweetness in his labour, no hope for him in the future. So much to heart did Basil take Annette's silence that, had his nature been inclined to evil instead of good, mischief to others would probably have ensued, but as it was he was the only sufferer. In his utterances, when he was drawn to speak of the shock he had received, he was apt to exaggerate matters and to present himself in the worst light, but there had fallen to his share an inheritance of moral goodness which rendered it impossible for him to become a backslider from the paths of rectitude and honour. Except that he

was unhappy in himself, and that Annette's
silence took the salt out of his days, he was
as he ever was, straightforward in his dealings
and gentle and charitable towards his fellow-
creatures.

"My dear, dear Basil" (thus ran Annette's
first letter, written about five months after
their last meeting in the Australian woods),
"I have tried ever so hard to write to you
before, but have not been able to because of
uncle and aunt. I was afraid if they found
out I was writing to you that they would
take the letter away or do something to prevent it reaching you, and I wanted, too, to
tell you how you could write to me, but
have never been able till now. You will be
glad to hear that if you write and address
your letters exactly as I tell you, I am almost
sure of receiving them. But first I must say
something about myself and how I am.
Uncle and aunt are not unkind to me, but
they are not kind. They leave me to myself
a good deal, but I know I am being watched
all the time. I don't mind that so much,
but what I do miss is my dear father's voice
and yours, and the birds and flowers and

beautiful scenery I always lived among till
I was taken away. I would not mind if you
were with me, for I love you truly, dear
Basil, and can never, never forget you. That
last time we were together by Mr. Corrie's
hut, how often and often do I think of it!
I go through everything that passed except
the unkind words spoken by Uncle Gilbert,
which I try not to remember. I must have a
wonderful memory, for everything you said
to me is as fresh now as though you had
just spoken them. Yes, indeed. Perhaps it
is because when we were on board ship I
used to sit on the deck, with my face turnèd
to Australia—the captain always pointed out
the exact direction—and go through it all in
my mind over and over and over again till I
got letter perfect. Shall I prove to you that
it is really so? Well, then, when I told you
I was afraid I was turning hard and bad
since Uncle Gilbert came to the plantation—
the dear old plantation!—you chided me so
gently and beautifully, and I promised never
to forget your words, knowing they would
keep me good. Then you said, 'Let them
keep you brave as well, my dear. I promise
to remember you always; to love you always,

and perhaps when you are a woman—it will
not be so long, Annette — we shall meet
again.' Well, Basil dear, I am waiting for
that time. I know it will not be yet, perhaps
not for years, but I can wait patiently, and I
shall always bear your words in mind. 'The
stars of heaven are not brighter than the
stars of hope and love we can keep shining in
our hearts.' Do you remember, Basil? And
then I asked you to kiss me, and said that
was the seal and that I should go away
happier. It comes to my mind sometimes
that your words are like flowers that never
die, and that grow sweeter and more beautiful every day. You could not have given me
anything better to make me happy. But I
must not keep going on like this or I shall
not have time to tell you some things you
ought to know.

"Well, then, Basil dear, we are not settled
anywhere, and if you were to come home
now (you call it home, I know, and so will I)
you would not know where to find me unless
you went to a place I will tell you of presently. First we came to London and
stopped there a little while, then we went to
Paris, then to Switzerland, and now we have

come back to London, where we shall remain
two or three weeks, and then go somewhere
else, I don't know where. Uncle Gilbert
never tells me till the day before, when he
says, ' We are going away to-morrow morning;
be ready.' So that by the time you receive
this letter we shall be I don't know where.
Uncle Gilbert is very fond of theatres, but he
has not taken me to one because he says
they are not proper places for girls. I daresay he is right, and I don't know that I want
to go, but aunt has been very dissatisfied
about it, as she is as fond of theatres as Uncle
Gilbert is. He used to go by himself, and
aunt would stop with me to take care of me,
but a little while ago, a day or two before we,
came back to London, they had a quarrel
about it. They did not notice that I was in
the room when they began, and when they
found it out they stopped. But I think it is
because of the quarrel that when we were in
London a young woman was engaged to travel
with us and to look after me when Uncle and
aunt are away. I am very glad for a good
many reasons. I am not very happy when
they are with me, and I breathe more freely
— or perhaps I think I do — when they

are gone. The young woman they have engaged is kind and good-natured, and I have grown fond of her already, and she has grown fond of me, so we get along nicely together. Her name is Emily Crawford, and she has a mother who lives in Bournemouth, a place by the sea somewhere in England. Her mother is a poor woman, and that is why Emily is obliged to go to service, but she is not a common person, not at all, and she has a good heart. She can read and write very well, and she picks up things quicker than I can. Of course you want to know why I speak so much of Emily, when I might be writing about myself. Well, it is very, very important, and it *is* about myself I am speaking when I am speaking of her.

"Basil, dear, it does one good to have some one to talk to quite freely and to open one's heart to. All the time I have been away, until this week, I have not had any person who would listen to me or who cared to speak of the happy years I spent on our dear plantation. Whenever I ventured to say a word about the past Uncle Gilbert put a stop to it at once by saying, 'There is no occasion to speak of it, you are living another

life now. Forget it, and everybody connected
with it.' Forget it! As if I could! But I do
not dare to disobey him. He is my guardian,
and I must be obedient to him. Aunt is just
the same, only she snaps me up when I say
anything that displeases her, while uncle
speaks softly, but he is as determined as she
is although they do speak so differently. I
do not know which way I dislike most—I
think both. So one night this week when
uncle and aunt were away, and I was reading, and Emily was sewing, she said to me,
'You have come from Australia, haven't you,
miss?' Oh, how pleased I was! I answered
yes, and then we got talking about Australia,
and I told her all about the plantation and
the life we led there, and all sorts of things
came rushing into my mind, and when I had
told her a great deal I began to cry. It was
then I found out Emily's goodness, for there
she was by my side wiping my tears away
and almost crying with me, and that is how
we have become friends. After that I felt
that I could speak freely to her, and I spoke
about you, of course. She promised not to
say a word to uncle or aunt, and I know I
can trust her. Now, Basil, dear, she has told

me how you can write to me and how I can
obtain your letters without uncle or aunt
knowing anything about it. Emily writes
home to her mother and receives letters from
her. If you will write and address your
letters to the care of Mrs. Crawford, 14,
Lomax Road, Bournemouth, England, Mrs.
Crawford will enclose them to Emily, who
will give them to me. Mrs. Crawford will
always know where Emily is while she remains
with me, which will be as long as she is allowed, Emily says, and I am sure to get your
letters. I feel quite happy when I think that
you will write to me, telling all about yourself. You said I was certain to make friends
in the new country I was going to, through
whom we should be able to correspond, and
although I would sooner do it through uncle
and aunt (but there is no possibility of that
because they do not like you), I feel there is
nothing very wrong in our writing to each
other in the way Emily proposes. So that is
all, and you will know what to do. I can
hardly restrain my impatience, but it is something very sweet to look forward to.

"I hope you found the locket with the
portrait of my dear mother in it. When we

see each other I shall expect you to show it
to me. If you see Mr. Corrie tell him that
the magpie is quite well, and that I can teach
him to say almost anything. Both uncle and
aunt have grumbled a good deal about the
bird, and would like me to get rid of it, but
that is the one thing—the only thing—that I
have gone against them in. 'I will be
obedient in everything else,' I said, 'but I
must keep my bird. You promised me.' So
they have yielded, and I have my way in
this at all events. It means a great deal to
me because I take care it shall not forget
your name. I keep it in my own room,
where they see very little of it, and it is only
when we are travelling that it is a trouble to
them.

"Now I must leave off, Basil dear. With
all my love, and hoping with all my heart that
we shall see each other when I am a little
older,—I remain, for ever and ever, your
loving friend,

"ANNETTE."

This letter interested and amused Newman
Chaytor. "She is a clever little puss," he
thought, "and will not be hard to impose

upon, for all her cunning. I wonder, I
wonder "—but what it was he wondered at
did not take instant shape ; it required some
time to think out. He replied to the letter,
addressing Annette as she directed. Although he knew it was not likely that Annette could be very familiar with Basil's
handwriting, he was as careful in imitating
it as he was in his letters to Basil's uncle ;
and as in the case of his letters to that old
gentleman, he kept a copy of the letters he
wrote to Annette. He was very careful in
the composition of his correspondence with
the young girl. He fell into the sentimental
mood, and smiled to think that the sentiments he expressed to Annette were just
those which would occur to Basil if he sat
down to write to her. " Basil would be
proud of me," he said, " if he read this letter.
It is really saving him a world of trouble,
and he ought to be grateful to me if it ever
come to his knowledge—which it never shall.
I will see to that." During the first year of
the progress of the vile plot the full sense of
the dangerous net he was weaving for himself
did not occur to him, and indeed it was only
by degrees that he became keenly conscious

of the peril attending its discovery. It made
him serious at first, but at the same time
more fixed in his resolve to carry it out to the
bitter end. Whatever it was necessary to do
he would do ruthlessly. Everything must
give way to secure his own safety, to insure
the life of ease and luxury he hoped to enjoy,
if all went well.

If all went well! What kind of sophistry
must that man use who, to compass his ends,
deems all means justifiable, without considering the misery he is ready to inflict upon
others in the pursuit upon which he is engaged? There lies upon some men's natures
a crust of selfishness so cruel that it becomes
in their eyes a light matter to transgress all
laws human and divine. They are blinded by
a moral obliquity, and think not of the hour
when the veil shall be torn from their eyes,
and when the punishment which surely waits
upon crime is meted out to them.

Annette's first letter to Basil is a fair
example of those which followed, except that
the progress of time seemed to deepen the
attachment she bore for him. In one letter
she sent a photograph of herself, and Newman Chaytor's heart beat high as he gazed

upon it. Annette was growing into a very lovely womanhood; beautiful, sweet, and gracious was her face; an angelic tenderness dwelt in her eyes.

"And this is meant for Basil," said Chaytor, in his solitude: and then exclaimed, as he contemplated the enchanting picture, "No! For me—for me!"

CHAPTER IV.

THE claim they were working proved very little richer than others they had taken up. They made certainly a few shillings a week more than was absolutely necessary to keep them in food and tobacco, and these few shillings were carefully husbanded by Chaytor, who was the treasurer of the partnership. Their departure was hastened by a meeting which did not afford Chaytor unalloyed pleasure. As he and Basil sat at the door of their canvas tent one summer night, who should stroll up to them but old Corrie.

"Here you are, then," cried the honest fellow.

"Why, Corrie!" exclaimed Basil, jumping to his feet, and holding out his hands.

"Master Basil," said old Corrie, grasping them cordially, "I am more than glad to see you. I was passing through, and hearing your tent was somewhere in this direction, I made up my mind to hunt you up. Well, well, well!"

"Here's my mate," said Basil, motioning to Chaytor, "you remember him."

"Oh yes," said old Corrie, nodding at Chaytor. "So you've been together all this time. What luck have you had?"

"Bad luck," answered Chaytor.

"Sorry to hear it. Never struck a rich patch, eh?"

"Never," said Chaytor. "And you?"

"I can't complain. To tell you the truth, I've made my pile."

"You have!" cried Chaytor, with a furious envy in his voice.

"I have. You made a mistake when you refused to go mates with me; I could have shown you a trick or two. However, that's past: what's ended can't be mended."

"What are you going to do now?"

"Haven't quite made up my mind. Think of going to Sydney for a spree; perhaps to Melbourne for another; perhaps shall give up that idea, and make tracks for old England. I've got enough to live upon if I like to take care of it. Well, Master Basil, I wish you had better news to give me. Have you heard

from the old country? No?" This was in
response to Basil's shake of the head. "Why,
I thought the little lady promised to write to
you."

"She did promise, but I have not heard for
all that."

"Out of sight, out of mind," observed
Chaytor, inwardly discomposed at the turn
the conversation had taken.

Old Corrie gave him a sour look. "I'll
not believe that of the little lady. The most
likely reason is that she has been prevented
by that old fox her uncle. Her silence must
have grieved you, Master Basil." Basil
nodded. "I know how your heart was set
upon her."

"Don't let's talk about it," said Basil, "it
is the way of the world."

"That may be," said old Corrie, regarding
Basil attentively, "but I'd have staked my
life that it wasn't the way of the little lady.
What has come over you? You're changed.
You were always brimming over with life and
spirits, and now you're as melancholy as a
black crow."

"I'm falling into the sere and yellow," said
Basil, with a melancholy smile.

"I can only guess at what you mean. You're getting old. Why, man alive, there's a good five-and-twenty year between you and me, and I don't consider myself falling into the what-do-you-call-'em! Pluck up, Master Basil. Here, let's have a little chat aside."

Chaytor gave Basil a look which meant, as plain as words could speak it, "Are you going to have secret conversations away from me after all the years we have been together, after all I've done for you?"

"Corrie," said Basil, laying one hand on old Corrie's arm and the other on Chaytor's, "if you've anything to say to me I should like you to say it before Chaytor. There's nothing I would wish to hide from him. He's been the truest friend to me a man ever had, and I owe him more than I can ever repay."

"Nonsense, Basil," said Chaytor with magnanimous humility; "don't say anything about it."

"But it ought to be said, and I should be the ungratefullest fellow living if I ever missed an opportunity of acknowledging it. I owe you something too, Corrie. There's that mare of yours I borrowed and lost."

" Shut up," growled old Corrie, " if you want us to part friends. I've never given the mare a thought, and as for paying me for it, well, you can't and there's an end of it. I'll say before your mate what is in my mind. You're a gentleman, Master Basil, and here you are wasting your time and your years to no purpose. England is the proper place for you." Chaytor caught his breath, and neither Basil nor old Corrie could have interpreted this exhibition of emotion aright; but Basil, who thought he understood it, smiled gently at Chaytor, as much as to say, " Don't fear ; I am not going to desert you." Old Corrie, who had paused, took up his words : " England is the proper place for you. Say the word, and we'll go together to Sydney and take two passages for home. There you can hunt up your old friends, and you'll be a man once more. Come now, say, ' Yes, Corrie,' and put me under an obligation to you for life."

"I can't say yes, Corrie, but I'm truly obliged to you for your kind offer. Even if I wished to break my connection with Chaytor—which I don't—it's for him to put an end to our partnership, not for me—don't you see that it would be impossible for me to lay myself under an obligation to you?"

"No, I don't see it," growled old Corrie.

"Then, again, Corrie, what inducement have I to return to England?"

"There's little lady," interrupted old Corrie.

"She has forgotten me," said Basil sadly. "What business have I to thrust myself upon her? If she desired to continue a friendship which was as precious to me as my heart's blood—yes, I don't mind confessing it; there may be weakness, but there is no shame in it —would she not have written to me? She would, if it was only one line. It is true that her uncle may be jealously guarding and watching her—there was no love lost between us—but in these three years that have passed since the last day we saw each other, it is not possible to think that she could not have contrived once to have put in the post a bit of paper with only the words, 'I have not forgotten you, Basil.' Who and what am I that I should cross the road she is traversing for the purpose of bringing a reminiscence to her mind that she chooses not to remember? There would not be much manliness in that.

Besides, it's a hundred chances to one that she's not in England at all. It is my belief she is living in her father's native country, Switzerland, where, surrounded by new scenes and new companions, I hope she is happy. Thank you again, Corrie; I cannot accept your offer."

"All right," said Corrie, with disappointment in his face and voice; "you ought to know your own mind, though I make bold to say I don't believe you've said what is in your heart. Well, there's an end of it. I'm off early in the morning. Good-bye, Master Basil."

"Good-bye, Corrie, and good luck to you."

"Good luck to *you*, better than you've had in more ways than one."

"Good-bye, Mr. Corrie," said Chaytor.

Old Corrie could scarcely refuse the hand that Chaytor held out to him, but the grasp he gave it was very different from the grasp he gave Basil's. Before he turned to leave the ill-assorted comrades he did something which escaped the eyes of Basil, but not those of Chaytor. He furtively dropped, quite close to Basil's feet, a round wooden matchbox, which, emptied of matches, gold-diggers fre-

quently used to fill with loose gold. Un-
observed by old Corrie, Chaytor put his foot
on the box and slipped it to the rear of himself. This was done while old Corrie was
turning to go. Basil was genuinely sorry to
see the last of his friend. Both the unexpected meeting and the leave-taking had a
touch of sadness in them which deeply affected
him, and he gazed with regret after the
vanishing form of the man who had offered
to serve him. This gave Chaytor an opportunity of slyly picking up the match-box; it
was weighty, and Chaytor knew that it was
filled with gold. "A bit of luck," he thought,
as he put the box in his pocket, "and a
narrow escape as well." He felt like a man
sitting on a mine which a stray match might
fire at any moment.

"Basil," he said, when old Corrie was out
of sight, "we will strike our tent to-morrow,
and go prospecting. I have a likely spot in
my mind."

"Very well," said Basil listlessly. "How
about money? Can we manage to get
along?"

"Oh, yes, we can manage."

Early in the morning the pegs which fastened the tent were dug out of the ground, the tent was rolled up and tied, and with heavy swags of canvas, blankets, tools, and utensils conveniently disposed about their persons, Basil and Chaytor set their faces to the south. They walked for two days, camping out at night, and halted at length on the banks of a river, the waters of which were low. In the winter the floods rolling down from the adjacent ranges made the river a torrent, covering banks which now were bare. These banks were of fine sand, and rising on each side for a distance of some thousands of yards were shelving mountains studded with quartz. Some eighteen months ago Basil and Chaytor had passed the place on their way to a new rush, and Chaytor thought it a likely place in which to find gold. They were now quite alone, not a living soul was within a dozen miles of them. They had reached the spot secretly, and their movements were unknown to any but themselves. Their nearest neighbours were on a cattle station some twelve or thirteen miles away.

"I have had an idea," said Chaytor, throwing the swag off his shoulders, an example which Basil followed, "for a long time past that somewhere about here gold was to be found. My plan is to prospect the place well, without any one being the wiser. Who knows? We may discover a new gold-field, and make our fortunes before we are tracked. Let us camp here, and try. We can't do much worse than we've done already."

"I'm agreeable to anything you propose," said Basil. "Let us camp here by all means."

"The great thing is, that nobody must be let into the secret. If we are discovered, 'Rush, O!' will be the cry, and we shall be overrun before we can say Jack Robinson."

"You have only to say what you wish, Chaytor. You have the cleverer head of the two. I hope for your sake we shall be successful."

"You don't much care for your own."

"Not much."

"You'll sing to another tune when we do succeed. It's wonderful how the possession of a lot of money alters one's view."

"I'll wait till I get it," said Basil sagely.

"The river runs low at this season, and there's no reason in the world why the sand banks shouldn't hold gold."

"They will hold it if it's there," said Basil, with a smile.

"We'll try the banks first because they are the easiest, and if we don't get gold in sufficient quantities there we'll try higher up the range. It's studded with quartz, and it looks the right sort. We'll put our tent up now, and in the morning we'll commence work— or rather you will commence work while I am away."

"Where are you going to?"

"There's grub to look after. We can't do without meat and flour. All we've got to live on at present is a tin of sardines, about half a pint of brandy, a little tea, and a couple of handfuls of buscuits. Now, I call that a coincidence."

"In what respect?"

"Do you forget," said Chaytor reproachfully, "the first night you came to Gum Flat? I gave you then pretty well all I had in the world in the shape of provisions, some biscuits, some sardines, and a flask of brandy."

"You did, old fellow, and that is the sum total of our provisions this evening." He shook Chaytor's hand warmly. "Don't think

me ungrateful, Chaytor, because I don't pro-
fess much.   Old Corrie said I was changed,
and I suppose I must be ; but I shall never
be so changed as to be unmindful of the way
you've stuck to me.   Yes, it is a coincidence.
But go on.   What do you mean to do about
grub, for I see you've something in your
mind ? "

"There's only one thing to do," said Chaytor.   " I must go to the cattle station to-night,
get there early in the morning, and buy
mutton and flour.   I shall have to look out
sharp that I'm not followed when I make my
way back again, but I think I can manage it.
I've done more difficult jobs than that."

"And you will be tramping the bush,"
said Basil, " while I remain at my ease here.
Why can't I go instead of you ? "

"Because," replied Chaytor, in a tone of
affectionate insistance, " as you have already
confessed, I am the cleverer of the two, and
because I have an idea, if we lose this chance,
that we shall never get another.   I don't
want you to be seen, Basil, that's the plain
truth of the matter.   You're not up to the
tricks of the men we meet.   Now, I am sly
and cunning——"

" You ? " interrupted Basil. " You are the soul of candour and honesty, Chaytor. No one else should say that of you while I stood by."

" I don't mean exactly what I said, Basil, but I am sure I can do the job more neatly than you could. As to the tramp through the bush, I think nothing of it, so let it be as I say."

Basil making no further objection, the tent was put up and a trench dug around to carry the rain away. Then a camp fire was made, and the water for tea boiled in a tin billy, after which they finished the biscuits and sardines.

" You will have to hold out till I come back," said Chaytor. " As I need not start till past midnight I'll turn in for an hour or two."

Shortly afterwards the comrades were wrapt in slumber, and the man with the evil conscience slept the sounder of the two. A little after midnight he rose, and without disturbing Basil, started for the cattle station. It was a warm starlit night, and he pondered upon matters as he made his way through the bush. Indeed, during the past two days he

had thought deeply of the situation in which
he was placed. Old Corrie's proposition to
take Basil to England had greatly alarmed
him, and had opened his eyes more clearly to
its gravity. It was this which had caused
him to hurry Basil away from the vicinity of
old Corrie, for it was quite likely that Corrie
would make another attempt to prevail upon
Basil before he took his departure, and the
second time Basil might yield. At all hazards
this must be prevented ; step by step he had
descended the abyss of crime, and it was too
late for him now to turn back. In entering
upon an evil enterprise men seldom see the
cost at which success must be purchased ;
it is only when they are face to face with
consequences that they tremble at their own
danger.

By daybreak Chaytor was at the cattle
station and had made his purchases ; by
noon he had rejoined Basil. His purchases
at the station had attracted no attention ; it
was a common enough proceeding, and now
they had food for a week. Fifteen miles
beyond the cattle station was a small township where they could also obtain supplies ; a
pilgrimage once a week to station or town-

ship would keep them going. In the township such gold as they obtained and wished to dispose of could also be turned into money. Thus, although they were quite alone, they were within hail of all that was necessary.

Shortly after Chaytor's return they set to work on the banks of the river. Basil showed his mate some pieces of quartz with fair-sized specks of gold in them, but Chaytor decided to try the river first, alluvial digging being so much easier. They found gold in the sand, and sufficient to pay, but not sufficient to satisfy Chaytor's cupidity. The result of a week's labour was between two and three ounces.

"This is better than we have done yet," said Basil.

"It is only the washings from the hills," said Chaytor, "and at any unexpected moment a flood of rain would swamp us. There are too many trees about to please me; wood draws water from the clouds. If we don't do better than this by the end of next week we'll mark out a claim on the range yonder, where the blue slate peeps out of the quartz."

Another journey had to be made for food,

and this time Chaytor went to the township, where he obtained what he required and sold exactly seven pennyweights of gold. He put on an appearance of great anxiety while the gold was being weighed, and sighed when the weight was announced. This was to throw the storekeeper off the scent; any considerable quantity of gold disposed of proudly would have excited suspicion of a Tom Tiddler's ground somewhere near, and Chaytor, had he so behaved, would certainly have been shadowed by men who were ever watchful for signs of the discovery of a new goldfield. It was in Chaytor's power to sell some fourteen ounces of gold had he been so inclined, for the match-box which old Corrie had furtively dropped at Basil's feet, and which Chaytor had slyly picked up unknown to his mate, contained twelve ounces of the precious metal, but he knew better than to attempt it. There was a post-office in the township, from which he dispatched a letter to the Sydney office, requesting that any letters lying there for Basil Whittingham might be forwarded on to him. He wrote and signed the order in Basil's name. He could not very well go to Sydney at present to fetch them ; there would be a risk in leaving Basil so long alone, for there being no coaches running from the township, the journey to Sydney and back could not be accomplished in less than nine or ten days. Easier to obtain the letters from England, if any arrived, by the means he adopted, and it was the easiest of tasks to keep the affair from the knowledge of Basil, who never dreamed of asking at any post-office whether there were any letters for him.

They worked a second week on the river-banks, at the end of which they had washed out over three ounces.

" An improvement," remarked Basil.

Chaytor shook his head discontentedly.

" Let us mark off a prospector's claim up the hill," he said. " We can always come back to the river."

This was done, and they commenced to sink. The difficulty they now encountered was the want of a windlass. Chaytor would not venture to purchase one in the township, whither he went regularly, being well aware that he could have done nothing that would more surely have drawn attention upon him. At odd times he bought some pieces of rope which he and Basil spliced till they had a length of about eighty feet. This rope, properly secured, enabled them to descend and ascend the shaft, foot-holes in the sides assisting them. The labour of digging a shaft in this manner was increased fourfold at least, but they could not be too cautious, Chaytor said. He remarked also that they seemed to be haunted by coincidences, and upon Basil asking for an explanation reproached him for his bad memory.

"How many of us were there upon Gum Flat," he said, "after your horse was stolen? Two. You and I alone. How many are there here? Two. You and I alone. When you fell down the shaft how did I get you up? By means of a rope secured at the top. How do we get up and down this shaft? By the same means. There was no windlass there; there is no windlass here. Don't you call these coincidences?"

"Yes," said Basil, "it is very singular."

"It would be very singular," thought Chaytor, "if you were at the bottom of this shaft one of these fine days and never got out of it alive. In that case coincidence would not hold good."

He drew a mental picture of the scene:
Basil helpless below, the rope lying loose on
the top, and he sitting by it waiting to assure
himself that the mate by whom he had dealt
so foully could never rise in evidence against
him. He saw this mental picture at the very
moment that Basil, with his sad earnest face,
was in sight.

In the shaft they were sinking they were
following a thin vein of gold-bearing quartz
which luckily for them was not devious in its
bearings, but ran down perpendicularly. It
was very narrow, not more than an inch in
width, but the deeper they sank the richer it
grew. The vein was more rubble than stone,
and the stuff was easily pounded and washed.
The first week they discovered it they
obtained four ounces of gold, the second week
seven, the third week twelve, the fourth and
fifth weeks the same, then there was a jump
to twenty ounces. They had reached a depth
of forty odd feet, and not a living being but
themselves had been seen near the spot.

This lucky break in their fortunes gave
Chaytor serious and discomforting food for
thought. He was convinced that their better
luck would continue for some time, and was

21*

almost sure that the thin vein they were
following would lead them to a richer and
wider reef. What would be the effect of
wealth upon Basil? Would it alter his views?
Would it turn his thoughts homewards? He
became hot and cold when this last thought
suggested itself, and that night he was visited
in his sleep by a dream so startling that he
jumped up in affright and sat in the dark
trembling like a leaf in a strong wind. He
dreamt that Basil had discovered his treachery, and had torn open his secret pocket in
which he kept not only the letters from
Annette and Basil's uncle he had received
from England, but the documents he had
stolen from Basil on Gum Flat, and the
locket which Annette had given to Basil at
their last meeting. "You monster!" Basil
had cried. "You have ruined my life and
shall pay the penalty!" It was at this point
that Chaytor awoke, trembling and in great
fear. Presently, when the pulses of his heart
beat more regularly, he heard Basil's soft
breathing. He struck a match, and rising
quietly looked down upon his comrade. The
young fellow was sleeping calmly, with no
thought of the evil genius standing over him.

Convincing himself that his stolen treasures were safe, Chaytor crept back to his stretcher, but he had little more sleep that night. His sense of security was shaken ; the earth was trembling beneath his feet.

CHAPTER V.

WHEN a man evilly inclined turns from the path of evil, it is generally because he fears for his own safety. He does not choose the straight road or relinquish a bad purpose from the awakening of the moral principle, but from a conviction that the deviation will best serve his own interests. In the initial stages of a bad scheme the prime mover seldom counts the cost; it is only when he is deeply involved that the consequences of his evil-doing stare him in the face, and warn him to halt. True repentance is rare; but there have been instances where a man, suddenly appalled by the enormity of his career of crime, conscientiously resolves to turn before it is too late, and to expiate, as far as lies in his power, for his misdeeds. There is something of heroism in this, and the sinner may hope for forgiveness at the divine throne, if not from human hands. Of such heroism Newman Chaytor was not capable. If he wavered, it was purely from selfish reasons, and because he saw before him a path in which lay greater chances of safety to himself. That he did waver is true, and the more wholesome and more merciful course which suggested itself to him was due, not to conscientious motives, but to circumstances quite independent of his original design. On the day following his disturbing dream he and Basil struck a wonderfully rich patch in the claim they were working. The stuff which was raised to the surface was literally studded with gold, and by nightfall they had washed out fifty ounces. The excitements of a gold-digger's life when fortune smiles upon him are all-absorbing. Marvellous possibilities dazzle and distort his mind; delirious visions rise to his imagination. In the early days of the goldfields it was a belief with numbers of miners that, at some time or other, gold would be discovered in such quantities that it could be hewn out like coal. A favourite phrase was, " We shall be able to cut it out with a cold chisel." Of course every man hoped that this wonderful thing would happen to him.

He held a chance in the lottery, and why should *he* not draw the grand prize which would astonish the world?

These possibilities flitted through Chaytor's mind as he and Basil sat at the door of their tent, smoking their pipes after their day's labour. The chairs they sat on were stumps of trees. Furniture they had none, inside their tent or out of it. For their beds they had gathered quantities of dry leaves, over which they spread a blanket, with another to roll themselves in. Rough living, but healthier than life in civilised cities. Early to bed and early to rise, plain food, moderate drinking, exercising their muscles for a dozen hours a day—all this was conducive to a healthy physical state. Their faces were embrowned, their limbs were hardened, their beards had grown long—they looked like men. This may be said of Chaytor as well as of Basil, for such play of expression as would have revealed the cunning of his nature was hidden by his abundant hair. A stranger, observing them, would have been astonished at the likeness of one to the other, and could have formed no other conclusion than that they were twin-born; but no stranger had seen them thus, for it was only during their late seclusion that Chaytor had copied Basil so exactly. Basil took but little note of this resemblance, and if he referred to it at all it was in a manner so slight as to show that he attached no importance to it. But it was seldom absent from Chaytor's mind; he had brooded constantly upon it, and had studied it as a lesson which, perfectly answered, was to bring with it the rich reward for which he had schemed.

"A good day's work," said Basil, holding out his hand for the tin dish which Chaytor held.

This tin dish contained the gold which they had gathered since sunrise, and Chaytor was turning it over with his knife. The moisture had dried out of it, and the gold lay loose. Chaytor passed the dish to Basil, who, in his turn, played with the shining metal with somewhat more than usual interest.

"Nearly as much," said Chaytor, "as we've got these last five weeks. It is a rare good day's work—if only it will last."

"That's the question," said Basil; "I should like to weigh it."

They entered the tent, and weighed the gold in the gold scales, which form part of a miner's working implements. It turned the fifty ounces.

"Honestly paid for," said Basil, "it represents a couple of hundred pounds. A hundred pounds each."

Chaytor merely nodded, and made no comment upon the remark, but it dwelt in his mind. Not so very long ago Basil had expressed indifference regarding their possession of gold, and had gone the length of saying that Chaytor might have his share, for all he cared for it. Now he expressed an interest in it, and reckoned their day's work at "a hundred pounds each." That indicated that he looked upon half as his fair share. What did this newly-awakened interest portend? With his instinctive cunning Chaytor felt that this was not a favourable time to open up the subject; far better to let it work quietly until it came to a natural head. Besides, he was feverishly engrossed in the question he had suggested, whether the rich patch they had struck would last. Time alone could answer that question. They retired to their beds of dry leaves a little earlier than usual, and were at work in the morning with the rising of the sun. Basil worked chiefly at the bottom of the shaft, Chaytor at the top, and the honest man of this ill-assorted pair sent up two buckets of stuff before breakfast, which was even richer than that they had raised on the previous day. Basil climbed to earth's surface hand over hand.

"He uses the rope like a cat," thought Chaytor.

The two buckets of stuff were emptied into a tub.

"Let us wash it out before breakfast," said Basil.

They went down to the river, carrying the tub between them. On the top of the auriferous soil were two tin basins, and, after puddling the tub well and letting the worthless refuse flow over the brim, they set to work, washing what remained in the basins, with that rotary motion in which gold-diggers are so skilful, and which enables them to get rid of the loosened earth, and keep the heavy precious metal at a safe angle in the bottom of the dish. It had hitherto been Basil's practice to leave this delicate operation to

Chaytor, but on this morning he took part in it, using one dish, while Chaytor used the other. Chaytor took note of every small circumstance ; nothing escaped him.

"This is a new move of yours, Basil," he said.

"I am beginning to take a real interest in the work," admitted Basil. "In a manner of speaking, it is waking me up."

"Glad to hear it," said Chaytor. "These two buckets are worth something. There's not less than twenty ounces."

There was more ; the stuff they had washed yielded twenty-three ounces, and the whole day's yield was worth four hundred pounds.

"Nothing to complain of now, Chaytor," observed Basil in the evening.

"Nothing." Basil was busy with paper and pencil. "What are you up to there ? Figuring ?"

"Yes," replied Basil. "I am reckoning how much four hundred pounds a day would bring us in at the end of the year. Here it is. Three hundred and twelve working days in the year, leaving Sundays free."

"Why should we do that ?" asked Chaytor.

"There's no one to see us. It would be a sheer waste of so much money."

Basil looked up in surprise; the remark was not agreeable to him, the tone in which it was spoken was still less so.

"I am old-fashioned perhaps," he said. "I do not choose to work on the Sabbath day."

"Growing particular."

"No; I have always held the same notion."

"We'll not argue. What is your reckoning?"

"Three hundred and twelve working days a year," continued Basil. "Twelve days for sickness, leaving three hundred. At four hundred pounds a day we get a total of a hundred and twenty thousand—in pounds. Sixty thousand pounds each. Truly, a great fortune."

"If it lasts," again said Chaytor.

"Of course, if it lasts. There's the chance of its getting better. How does it look to you—as if it will hold out?"

Chaytor had been down the claim for some hours during the day, and had pocketed between forty and fifty ounces, which he

chose to regard as his own especial treasure
trove.

"There's no saying," he said. "The vein
runs sideways into the rock. It may peg out
at any moment."

"We shall not have done badly by the
time it does. I have to thank you for
bringing me here."

"Yes," said Chaytor, ungraciously; "it
was my discovery. Don't forget that."

"I shall never forget it, Chaytor, nor any
of the other good turns you have done me.
I don't know whether it is a healthy or an
unhealthy sign that this better luck should
have aroused me from the apathy in which I
have been so long plunged. It has softened
me; the crust of indifference, of disbelief in
human goodness, is melting away, I am glad
to say. That this is due to the prospect of
becoming rich is not very creditable; I would
rather that the change in me had sprung
from a less worldly cause; it would have
made me better satisfied with myself. But
we mortals are very much of the earth,
earthy, and we take too readily the impressions of immediate circumstance and of our
surroundings. They mould our characters,

as it were, and change them for better or worse."

" You can do a lot of thinking in a little time, Basil."

" How so, Chaytor ? "

" Because yesterday you were black, to-day you are white. Yesterday it was a bad world ; to-day it is a good one. A rapid transformation, savouring somewhat of fickleness."

" A just reproof, but I cannot alter my nature. I have never given myself credit for much stability except in my affections, and there, I think, I am constant. As you say, a little reflection has effected a great change in me. We judge the world too much from our own stand-point. We are fortunate, we trust and are not deceived, we love and are loved in return, our daily labour is rewarded —it is a good world, a bright world. We are unfortunate, we trust and are de-ceived, we love and are not loved in return, we toil and reap dead leaves—it is a bad world, a black world. That is the way with us."

" All of which wise philosophy has sprung from our discovery of a rich patch of gold."

"I am afraid I can ascribe these better and juster feelings to no other cause."

"Basil," said Chaytor, toying with his pipe and tobacco, "say that your reckoning should be justified by results. Say that we work here undiscovered for a year—for there is the contingency of our being tracked to be thought of——"

"Of course."

"Say that we do not fall ill or meet with an accident which disables us, say that to-day is but a sample of all the other days to follow in the next twelve months, say that we make a hundred thousand pounds, what would you do with your share? For I suppose," said Chaytor, with a light laugh, "that the offer you once made of letting me keep the lot if we struck gold rich, is now withdrawn."

"I am properly reproved. Yes, Chaytor, I should expect my share." Basil said this in a rather shamefaced voice. "It proves in the first place that I am not a very dependable fellow, and in the second place it proves my philosophy, that we are moulded by immediate circumstances."

"Oh, it is natural enough; I never expected to meet with a man who would step out of the ordinary grooves. There are temptations which it is impossible to resist, and you and I are no different from the rest of mankind."

"I should place you above the majority, Chaytor."

"I am obliged to you, but I am as modest as yourself, and cannot accept the distinction. Well, Basil, say that everything happened as I have described, what would you do at the end of the year, with its wonderful result of overflowing purses?" Basil was silent, and Chaytor continued: "You said once that you intended to live and die in the colonies. Do you stick to that?"

"No."

"What would you do?"

"I should return to England."

Chaytor shivered. This good fortune, then, which he had bestowed upon Basil, was to be the means of his own destruction. Basil in England, nothing could prevent his treachery being discovered. He had led to his own ruin. With assumed unconcern he asked:

"For any specific purpose, Basil?"

"It has dawned upon me, Chaytor, that in

my thoughts I may have done injustice to one
whom I loved and who loved me."

" The little girl, Annette ? "

" The little girl, Annette."

" But, speaking of love as you do, one
would suppose that she was a woman.
Whereas she was a mere child when you last
saw her."

" That is true, and I speak of her only as
a child.   Chaytor, there was something so
sweet in Annette's nature, that she grew in
my heart as a beloved sister might have
done.   To that length I went ; no farther.
Have you ever felt the influence of a child's
innocent love ?   It purifies you ; it is a charm
against evil thoughts and evil promptings.
Annette's affection was like an amulet lying on
my heart."

" Your   object   in   returning   to   England
would be to seek her out ? "

" I   should   endeavour   to   find   her.   Her
silence may have been enforced.   She may
be unhappy ; I might be of service to her.
There are other reasons.   I seem in this far-
off country to be cut off from sympathy,
from humanizing influences.   The life does
not suit me.   A man, after all, is not a stone ;

he has duties, obligations, which he should endeavour to fulfil. You have heard me speak of my uncle. He was kind to me for a great many years, up to the point of my offending him. He is old: consideration is due to him. I should go to him and say, 'I do not want your money; give it to whom you will, but let us be friends.'"

"A hundred to one that he would show you the door," said Chaytor, who found in these revelations more than sufficient food for thought.

"At all events, I should have done my duty; but I think you are mistaken. He has a tender heart under a rough exterior, and was always fond of me, even, I believe, when he cast me off. I should not wonder if he has not sometimes thought, 'Why did Basil take me at my word? Why did he not make advances towards me?' He would be right in so thinking; I ought to have striven for a reconcilement. But I was as obstinate as he was himself, and perhaps prouder because I was poor. In a sort of way I defied him, and as good as said I could do without him. I was wrong; I should have acted differently.

"You seem to me, Basil," said Chaytor,

22*

slowly, " to fall somewhat into the same error in speaking of him as you do when you speak of Annette. You speak of the little girl as if she was a woman; you speak of your uncle as if he is living."

" If he is dead I should learn the truth."

" I suppose that you would not leave the colony unless you were rich ? "

" I think not ; I should be placing myself in a false position. We will not talk of it any more to-night, Chaytor. I am tired and shall get to bed.

" So shall I. The conversation has been a bit too sentimental for me. Besides, when you say that you are cut off from sympathy and human influences here, you are not paying me a very great compliment, after the sacrifices I have made for you. But it is the way of the world."

" Why, Chaytor," said Basil, with affectionate emphasis, " I never proposed that we should part. My hope was that we should go home together. You are as much out of place here as I am. With your capacities and with money in your pocket, you could carve a career in England which would make you renowned."

" It is worth thinking of ; but I must have your renewed promise, Basil, that you will not throw up our partnership here till we have made our fortune."

"I give you the promise. It would be folly to land in the old country penniless."

" So that the upshot of it is, that it all depends upon money. In my opinion everything in life does."

" You do yourself an injustice, and are not speaking in your usual vein. I daresay I am to blame for it. Forgive me, friend."

" Oh, there's nothing to forgive ; but it is strange, isn't it, that the first difference we have had should have sprung from the prospect of our making our pile ? Good night, old fellow."

" Good night, Chaytor."

CHAPTER VI

CHAYTOR lay awake that night, brooding.
He found himself on the horns of a dilemma,
and all the cunning of his nature was needed
to meet the difficulty and overcome it successfully. The scheme he had laid, and very
nearly matured, had been formed and carried
out in the expectation that the run of ill
luck which had pursued him on the goldfields
would continue. But now the prospect was
suddenly altered. Gold floated before his
eyes; he saw the stuff in the claim they
were working more thickly studded than ever
with the precious metal; extravagant as were
the calculations which Basil had worked out
they were not too extravagant for his imagination, and certainly not sufficiently extravagant for his cupidity. There was no reason
in the world why these anticipations should
not be more than fulfilled. Fabulous fortunes
had been realised on the goldfields before

to-day—why should not the greatest that had ever been made be theirs? He was compelled to take Basil into this calculation. He could not work alone in the claim; a mate was necessary, and where should he find one so docile as Basil? With all his heart he hated Basil, who seemed to hold in his hands the fate of the man who had schemed to destroy him. Luck had changed and the end he had in view must be postponed, must even, perhaps, be ultimately abondoned. To turn his back upon the fortune within his grasp for a problematical fortune in the old country was not to be dreamt of. The bird he had in hand was worth infinitely more than the two he had in the bush—these two being Annette and Basil's uncle. The result of his cogitations was that the scheme upon which he had been engaged should remain in abeyance until it was proved whether the gold they had struck in their claim was a flash in the pan, or would hold out till their fortunes were made. In the former case he would carry out his scheme to the bitter end; in the latter he would amass as much money as he could, and then fly to America, where life would be almost as enjoyable as in England. It was hardly likely, if Basil discovered his treachery, that he would follow him for the mere purpose of revenge. " He is not vindictive," thought the rogue ; " he is a soft-hearted fool, and will let me alone." Thus resolved, Chaytor waited for events. It is an example of the tortuous reasoning by which villainy frequently seeks to justify itself that Chaytor threw from his soul the responsibility of a contemplated crime, by arguing that the result did not depend upon him but upon nature. If the claim proved to be as rich as they hoped, Basil would be spared ; if the gold ran out, he must take the consequences. Having thus established that circumstance would be the criminal, the evil-hearted man disposed himself for sleep.

He had not long to wait to decide which road he was to tread. During the week they learned that their anticipations of wealth were not to be realised. Each bucket of earth that was sent up from the shaft became poorer and poorer, and from the last they obtained but a few grains of gold. The following day they met with no better fortune ; the rich patch was exhausted ; the pocket in which they had found the gold was empty.

"Down tumble our castles," said Basil, with a certain bitterness.

"We may strike another rich patch," said Chaytor, and thought, "I will not wait much longer. I am sick of fortune's freaks; I will take the helm again, and steer my ship into pleasure's bay."

He went to the township, openly for provisions and secretly to see if there was any news from England. There were letters at the Post Office awaiting Basil Whittingham, Esq. Chaytor put them in his pocket without opening them, purchased some provisions, and set forth to rejoin Basil. He was more careful in his movements than he had ever been. He had a premonition that the unopened letters contained news of more than ordinary importance, and if he were tracked and followed now his plans would be upset and all the trouble he had taken thrown away. Basil and he were hidden from the world; no one knew of their whereabouts, no person had any knowledge of their proceedings. Should Basil disappear, who would suspect? Not a soul. Basil had not a friend or acquaintance in all the colonies who was anxious for his safety or would be curious to know what had become of him.

Midway between the township at which he had obtained Basil's letters and the claim which had animated him with delusive hopes the schemer halted for rest. He listened and looked about warily to make sure that no one had followed him. Not a sound fell upon his ears, no living thing was within hail. There are parts of the Australian woods which are absolutely voiceless for twenty-three out of every twenty-four hours. This one hour, maybe, is rendered discordant by the crows, whose harsh cries grate ominously upon the ear. At the present moment, however, these pestilential birds were far away, and satisfied that there was no witness of his proceedings, Chaytor threw himself upon the earth and opened the letters. The first he read was from the lawyers, who had already written to Basil in reply to the letters his false friend had forged. It was to the following effect :—

"DEAR SIR,

"We write at the request of your uncle, Mr. Bartholomew Whittingham, who, we regret to say, is seriously ill. He desires us to inform you that he has abandoned the intention as to the disposition of his property with which he made you acquainted before your departure from England. A will has been drawn out and duly signed, constituting you his sole heir. Ordinarily this would not have been made known to you until the occurrence of a certain event which appears imminent, but our client wished it otherwise, and as doctors happily are not invariably correct in their prognostications it may happen that you will yet be in time to see him if you use dispatch upon the receipt of this communication, and take ship for England without delay. To enable you to do this we enclose a sight draft upon the Union Bank of Australia for five hundred pounds, and should advise you to lose not a day in putting it to the use desired by our client. It is our duty at the same time to say that we hold out no hope that you will arrive in time. In the expectation of seeing you within a reasonable period, and receiving your instructions, we have the honour to remain,

"Your obedient servants,

"BULFINCH & BULFINCH."

There was another letter from the lawyers:

" DEAR SIR,

" Following our letter of yesterday's date
we write to say that we have been directed
by your uncle, Mr. Bartholomew Whittingham, to forward to you the sealed enclosure
which you will find herewith. We regret to
inform you that our client is sinking fast, and
that the doctors who are attending him fear
that he cannot last through the week.

" We have the honour to remain,
" Your obedient servants,
" BULFINCH & BULFINCH."

Before unfastening the " sealed enclosure,"
Chaytor rose in a state of great excitement, and
allowed his thoughts to find audible expression:

"At last! Here is the certainty. No more
Will-o'-the-wisps. Fortune is mine—do you
hear?—mine. Truly, justly mine. Who has
worked for it but I? Tell me that. Would
the idiot Basil ever have humbled himself as
I did; would he ever have worked his old
uncle as I have done? What is the result?
I softened the old fellow's heart, and the
money he would have left to some charity has

fallen to me. Every labourer is worthy of his
hire, and I am worthy of mine. Basil would
never have had one penny of the fortune, and
therefore it is my righteous due. At last, at
last! No more sweating and toiling. The
world is before me, and I shall live the life of
a gentleman. There is work still to be done,
both here and at home, and *I will do it*.
No blenching, Chaytor; no flinching now.
What has to be done *must* and *shall* be done.
There is less danger in making the winning
move than in upsetting the board after the
game I have played. Hurrah! Let me see
what the precious 'enclosure' has to say for
itself."

He broke the seal, and read:

" MY DEAR NEPHEW BASIL,

" My sands of life are running out, and
before it is too late I write to you, probably
for the last time. You will be glad to hear
from me direct, I know, for your nature is
different from mine, and your heart has
always been open to tender impressions.
When I cast you from me I dare say you
suffered, but after my first unjust feeling of
resentment was over my sufferings have been

far greater than yours could have been. It
is the honest truth that in abandoning you I
abandoned the only real pleasure which life
had for me ; but my obstinacy, dear lad,
would not allow me to take steps towards a
reconcilement. It may be that had you done
so I should still have hardened my heart
against you, and should have done you the
injustice of thinking that you wished to pro-
pitiate me for selfish motives. In these, as I
believe them to be, the last hours of my life,
I have no wish to spare myself ; I can see
more clearly now than I have done for many
a long year, and my pride deserves no excuse.
This 'pride' has been the bane of my life ; it
has sapped the fountains of innocent enjoyment ; it has enveloped me in a steel shroud
which shut me out from love and sympathy.
You, and you alone, since I was a young
man, were able to penetrate this shroud, and
even to you I showed only that worse side of
myself by which the world must have judged
me. I did not give myself the trouble of
inquiring whether the counsel I was instilling
into you was true or false ; I see now that it
was false, and it is some comfort to me to
know that your nature was too simple and

honourable, too loving and sympathetic, to
be warped by it. Early in life I met with a
disappointment which soured me. There is
no need to inscribe that page in this letter—a
loving letter, I beg you to believe. It was a
disappointment in love, and from the day I
experienced it I became soured and em-
bittered. I was a poor man at the time, and
I devoted myself to the task of making
money; I made it, and much good has it
done me. With wealth at my command I set
up two dark starting points, which I allowed
to influence me in every question under consideration — one, money, the other human
selfishness. These, with a dogged and obstinate belief in the correctness of my own
judgment on every matter which came before
me, made me what I have been. I had no
faith, I had no religion; my life was godless,
and the attribute of selfishness which I
ascribed to the actions of all other men
guided and controlled me in mine. You
never really saw me in my true character.
That I regarded money as the greatest good
I did not conceal from you, but other sides of
me, even more objectionable than this, were
not, I think, revealed to you. The mischief

I would have done you glanced off harmlessly, as the action you took in ruining yourself to pay your father's debts proved. You were armed with an invincible shield, my dear lad, a shield in which shone the religious principle, honourable conduct, and faith in human nature. Be thankful for that armour, Basil; it is not every man who is so blessed. And let me tell you this. It is often an inheritance, and if not that, it is often furnished by a mother's loving teaching and influence. You had the sweetest of mothers; mine was of harder grain. I lay no blame upon her, nor, I repeat, do I seek to excuse myself, but I would point out to you, as a small measure of extenuation, that some of us are more fortunate than others in the early training we receive, and in the possession of inherited virtues.

"Basil, my dear lad, you did right in paying your father's debts, despite the base view I expressed of your action. Angry that a step so important should have been taken without my consent being asked, angry, indeed, that it should have been taken at all, I said to myself, 'I will punish him for it; I will teach him a lesson.' So I wrote you a

heartless letter, informing you that I had
resolved to disinherit you, and suggesting
that you should return the money I had
freely given you and which was justly yours.
There are few men in the world who would
have treated that request as you did, and
you could not have dealt me a harder blow
than when you forwarded me a cheque for
the amount, with interest added. Your independence, your manliness, hardened instead
of softened me; 'He does it to defy me,' I
thought, and I allowed you to leave England
under the impression that the ties which had
bound us together were irrevocably destroyed.
But the blow I aimed at you recoiled upon
myself; your reply to my mean and sordid
request has been a bitter sting to me, and
had you sought to revenge yourself upon me
you could not have accomplished your purpose more effectually. I have always lived a
lonely life, as you know; since I lost you my
home has been still more cheerless and lone-
some; but I would not call you back—no,
my pride stopped me; I could not endure the
thought that you, or any man, should triumph
over me. You see, my boy, I am showing
you the contemptible motives by which I was

actuated; it is a punishment I inflict upon
myself, and I deserve the harshest judgment
you could pass upon me. If my time were to
come over again, would I act differently? I
cannot say. A man's matured character is
not easily twisted out of its usual grooves. I
am as I have been made, or, to speak more
correctly, as I chose to make myself, and I
have been justly punished.

"But, Basil, if the harvest I have gathered
has been worthless to me and to others, some
good may result from it in the future. Not
at my hands, at yours. You are my sole heir,
and you will worthily use the money I leave
you. I look forward to the years to come,
and I see you in a happy home, with wife
and children around you, and it may be then
that you will give me a kind thought and
that you will place a flower on my grave.

"I am greatly relieved by this confession.
Good-bye, my lad, and God bless you.

"Your affectionate Uncle,

"BARTHOLOMEW WHITTINGHAM."

"Sentimental old party," mused Newman
Chaytor, as he replaced the letter in its envelope. "If this had fallen into Basil's hands

it would have touched him up considerably. The old fellow had to give in after all, but it was my letters that worked the oracle. The credit of the whole affair is mine, and Mr. Bartholomew Whittingham ought to be very much obliged to me for soothing his last hours." He laughed — a cruel laugh. "As for the harvest he has gathered, I promise him that it shall be worthily spent. He sees in the future his heir in a happy home, with wife and children around him. Well! — perhaps. If all goes smooth with the charming Annette, we'll see what we can do to oblige him. Now let me read the little puss's letter; there may be something interesting in it."

"My dear Basil" (wrote Annette), "I have something to tell you. Uncle Gilbert has discovered that we have been corresponding with each other, and there has been a scene. It came through aunt. The day before yesterday they went out and left me and Emily together. From what they said I thought they would have been gone a good many hours, and I got out my desk and began to read your letters all over again. Do you

23*

know how many you have written me?
Seven; and I have every one of them, and
mean to keep them always. After reading
them I sat down to write to you—a letter
you will not receive, because this will take
its place, and because I had not written a
dozen words before aunt came in suddenly,
and caught me bending over my desk. Seeing her, I was putting my letter away (I
never write to you when she is with me)
when she came close up to me and laid her
hand on mine. 'What is that you are
writing?' she asked. 'A letter,' I replied.
It was not very clever of me, but I did not
for the moment know what other answer to
give. 'To whom?' she asked. 'To a friend,'
I said. 'Oh, you have friends,' she said;
'tell me who they are.' 'I have only one,' I
said, 'and I am writing to him.' 'And he
has written to you?' she said. 'Yes,' I said,
'he has written to me.' 'Who is this only
friend?' she asked; 'do I know him?' 'Yes,'
I said, 'you knew him slightly. There is no
reason for concealment; it is Basil, my dear
father's friend.' 'Oh,' she said, 'your dear
father's friend. Is he in England, then?'
'No,' I answered, 'he is in Australia.' 'His

letters should have been addressed to the care of your uncle,' she said, ' and that, I am sure, has not been the case, or they would have passed through our hands. How have you obtained them?' 'It is my secret,' I replied. Fortunately Emily was not in the room, and I do not think they have any suspicion that she has been assisting me; if they had they would discharge her, though I should fight against that. 'Your answers are evasive,' she said. 'They are not, aunt,' I said; 'they are truthful answers.' 'Are you afraid,' she asked, 'if the letters had been addressed to our care, as they ought to have been, that they would not have been given to you?' I did not answer her, and she turned away, and said she would inform Uncle Gilbert of the discovery she had made. I did not go on with my first letter to you when she was gone; I thought I would wait till Uncle Gilbert spoke to me. He did the same evening. 'Your aunt has informed me,' he said, ' that you have been carrying on a correspondence with that man named Basil, who so very nearly imposed upon your father in Australia.' 'That man, uncle,' I said, 'is a gentleman, and he did not try to impose upon my father.'

'It will be to your advantage, my dear niece,' said Uncle Gilbert, very quietly, 'not to bandy words with me, nor say things which may interfere with your freedom and comfort. I am your guardian, and dispute it as you may, I stand in your father's place. To carry on a clandestine correspondence with a young man who is no way related to you is improper and unmaidenly. May I inquire if there is any likelihood of your correspondent favouring us with a visit?' 'I hope I shall see him one day,' I said. 'There is a chance of it then,' he said, 'and you can probably inform me when we may expect him.' 'No, I cannot tell you that,' I said. 'Your aunt believes,' he said, 'that you are not speaking the truth when you answer questions we put to you.' 'All my answers are truthful ones,' I said. 'You refuse to tell us,' he said, 'by what means this secret correspondence has been carried on.' 'I refuse to tell you,' I answered. 'I will not press you,' he said, 'but it will be my duty to discover what you are hiding from me. I shall succeed, I never undertake a task and fail. I always carry it out success- fully to the end. In the meantime this correspondence must cease.' 'I will not

promise,' I said, 'anything I do not mean to
fulfil.' 'That is an honest admission,' he said,
'and I admire you for it. Nevertheless, the
correspondence must cease, and if you persist
in it I shall find a way to put a stop to it.
Your reputation, your good name is at stake,
and I must guard you from the consequences
of your imprudence. My dear niece, I fear
that you are bent upon opposing my wishes.
It is an unequal battle between you and me—
I tell you so frankly. You are under my
control, and I intend to exercise my authority.
We will now let the matter drop.' And it did
drop there and then, and not another word
has been spoken on the subject.

"There, Basil, I have told you everything
as far as I can recollect it. I might be much
worse off than I am. But it would be different if I did not have you to think of, if
I did not feel that I have a dear, dear friend
in the world, though he is so many thousands
of miles away, and that some day I shall see
him again. It is something to look forward
to, and not a day passes that I do not think
of it. You remember the books you used to
tell me of on the plantation. I have read
them all again and again, and they are all

delightful. If the choice were mine, and you were to be near me, or with me as my dear father wished, I should dearly like to live the old life on the plantation; but there would be a difference, Basil; I could not live it now without books, and I do not see how anybody could. Often do I believe them to be real, and when I have laid down one which has made me laugh and cry I feel as if I had made new friends with whom I can rejoice and sympathise. There will be plenty to talk of when we meet, for that we shall meet some day I have not the least doubt. Only if you would grow rich, and come home soon, it would be so beautiful. Really and truly, Basil, I want a friend, a true friend to talk to about things. 'About what things, Annette?' perhaps you ask. How shall I explain? I will try—only you must remember that I am older than when we were together on the plantation, and that, as Uncle Gilbert implied, in a year or two I shall be a woman.

"Basil, when that time comes I want to have more freedom than I have now; I do not want to feel as if I were in chains; but how shall I be able to set myself free without a friend like you by my side? I do not

think I am clever, but one can't help thinking
of things.   I understand that when my dear
father died Uncle Gilbert was doing what he
had a right to do in becoming my guardian
and taking care of the money that was left.
Emily says it is all mine, but I do not know.
If it is, I should be glad to give half of it to
Uncle Gilbert if he would agree to shake
hands with me and bid me good-bye.   We
should be ever so much better friends apart
from each other.   I did venture timidly to
speak to him once about my dear father's
property, but he only said, 'Time enough,
time enough ; there is no need to trouble
yourself about it ; wait till you are a good
many years older.'   But, Basil, I want to be
free before I am a good many years older,
and how is that to be managed without your
assistance ?   That is what I mean when I
say I want a true friend to talk about things.

"I must leave off soon ; Emily says the
mail for Australia leaves to-day, and this letter has to be posted.   I am writing it very
early in the morning in my bedroom, before
uncle and aunt are up ; it is fortunate that
they do not rise till late.   But to be compelled to write in this way—do you under-

stand now what I mean when I say that I do not want to feel as if I were in chains? Emily says she will manage to post the letter for me without uncle and aunt knowing, and I hope she will be able to. Of course it would be ridiculous for me to suppose that Emily and I can be a match for Uncle Gilbert, for I am certain he is watching me, though there is no appearance of it. The way he talks and the way he looks sometimes puts me in mind of a fox.

"Good-bye, Basil. Do not forget me, and if you do not hear from me for a long time do not think I have forgotten you. I can never, never, do that. Oh, how I wish time would pass quickly!

"Always yours affectionately,

"ANNETTE."

When he finished reading Annette's letter Newman Chaytor looked at the date, and saw that it had been written a month earlier than the letter from the lawyers. Examining the post-mark on the envelope he saw that it could not have been posted till three weeks after it had been written, and that it bore a French stamp.

"The little puss was not in England," he

thought, "when she contrived to get this letter popped into the post. That shows that she was right in supposing that Uncle Gilbert was watching her. Sly old fox, Uncle Gilbert. He means to keep tight hold of the pretty Annette. Saint George to the rescue! I feel quite chivalrous, and as if I were about to set forth to rescue maidens in distress. She is not quite devoid of sense, this Annette; it will be an entertainment to have a bout with Uncle Gilbert on her behalf. He saw very little of Basil, and if we resembled each other much less than we do it would be scarcely possible for him to suspect that another man was playing Basil's part in this rather remarkable drama. Time, circumstance, everything is in my favour—but I wish the next few weeks were over.".

The harsh cawing of crows aroused him from his musings. Their grating voices were a fit accompaniment to his cruel thoughts. With a set, determined face, and with a heart in which dwelt no compunction for the deed he was about to do, he turned his face towards the spot where Basil, unsuspicious of the fate in store for him, was awaiting the comrade in whom he had put his trust.

CHAPTER VII.

In Australia, as in all new countries where treasure is discovered or where land is not monopolised by the few, townships spring up like mushrooms. Some grow apace, and become places of importance; others, in which the promise which brought them into existence is unfulfilled, languish and die out, to share the fate of the township of Gum Flat, in which Basil had met the man who played him false. Shortly after the events which have been recorded, a party of prospectors halted in a valley some eight miles from the river where Basil and Newman Chaytor had been working, and began to look for gold. Their search was rewarded, the precious metal was found in paying quantities, and miners flocked to the valley and spread themselves over the adjacent country. The name of one of the early prospectors was Prince, and a township being swiftly formed, there was a certain

fitness in dubbing it Princetown. All the
adjuncts of a town which bade fair to be
prosperous were soon gathered together. At
the heels of the gold-diggers came the storekeepers, with tents in which to transact their
business, and drayloads of goods wherewith
to stock their stores. The tide, set going,
flowed rapidly, and in less than a fortnight
Princetown was a recognised centre of the
rough civilisation which reigns in such-like
places. Storekeepers, publicans, auctioneers,
plied their trade from morning till night, and
the gold, easily obtained, was as easily parted
with by the busy bees, who lived only for
the day and thought not of the morrow.
The scene, from early morning till midnight,
was one of remarkable animation, replete
with strange features which a denizen of old-
time civilisation, being set suddenly in its
midst, would have gazed upon with astonish-
ment. Here was a cattle-yard, in which
horses for puddling machines and drays, and
sheep and oxen for consumption, were being
knocked down to the highest bidder during
ten hours of the day. A large proportion of
the horses purchased by the miners were
jibbers and buckjumpers, and a very Babel

of confusion reigned in the High Street as
they strove to lead away their purchases.
Around each little knot of mates who had
bought a jibber or a buckjumper a number
of idlers gathered, shouting with derision or
approval when the horse or the man was
triumphant. Exciting struggles between the
two were witnessed ; men jumped upon
unsaddled horses and were thrown into the
air amid the yells of the spectators, only to
jump on again and renew the contest. Here
an attempt was being made to pull along a
jibber, whose forelegs were firmly planted
before it, while twenty whips were being
cracked at its heels to urge it on in the desired direction. A dozen yards off, up and
out went the heels of a buckjumping brute,
scattering the crowd, and for a moment vic-
torious. Nobody was seriously hurt, bruises
being reckoned of no account by these wanderers from the home-land, who for the first
time in their lives were breathing the air of
untrammelled freedom. It was wonderful to
observe the effects of the newer life which
was pulsing in the veins of the adventurers.
At home they would have walked to and
from their work, or idled in the streets be-

cause work was not to be obtained, listless
and spiritless, mere commonplace mortals
with pale faces, and often hopeless eyes.
Here it was as if fresh, vigorous young blood
had been infused into them. The careless,
easy dress, the manly belt with its fossicking
knife in sheath, the ragged and graceful billy-
cock hat, the lissome movements of their
limbs, the hair flowing upon their breasts,
transformed them from drudges into something
very like heroes. Seldom anywhere in the
world can finer specimens of manhood be
seen than on these new goldfields; it is impossible to withhold admiration of the manlier
qualities which have sprung into life with the
free labour in which their days are engaged.
It is true that liberty often degenerates into
lawless licence, but the vicious attributes of
humanity must be taken into account, and
they are as conspicuous in these new scenes,
mayhap, as in the older grooves; and although
crime and vice are met with, their proportion
is no larger—indeed, it is not so large—than
is made manifest by statistics in the older
orders of civilisation. Next to the cattle
sale-yard is a small store in which the wily
gold-buyer is fleecing and joking with the

miner who comes to change virgin gold into
coined sovereigns or the ragged bank notes
of Australian banks.   Next to the gold-
buyer's tent is a stationer who, for the modest
sum of half-a-crown, will give a man an envelope, a sheet of notepaper, and pen and ink,
with which he can write a letter to a distant
friend.   It was an amazing charge, but it was
not uncommon during the first few weeks of
life on a new goldfield, and the wonder of it
was that men who toiled in the old countries
for little more than half-a-crown a day slapped
down the coin without a murmur against the
extortion.   Next to the stationer was a canvas
hotel, wherein thimblefuls of brandy and
whiskey were retailed at a shilling the nobbler,
and Bass's pale ale at two shillings the pint
bottle.   Then clothes stores, provision stores,
general stores, dancing and billiard saloons,
branches of great banks, with flags waving
over their fronts, and all driving a roaring
trade.   The joyousness of prosperity was
apparent in every animate sign that met the
view, and a rollicking freedom of manner
was established, very much as if it were an
order of freemasonry which made all men
brothers.   Here was a man who in England

never had three sovereigns to " bless himself with " (a favourite saying, which has its meaning) calling upon every person in sight —strangers to him, every man Jack of them —to come and drink at his expense at the usual shilling a thimbleful, throwing to the bar-tender a dirty banknote, and pocketing the change without condescending to count it. At present the circulation was confined to bank notes, sovereigns and silver money. Coppers were conspicuous by their absence, and, falling into miners' hands, would very likely be pitched away with scorn. The lowest price for anything was sixpence, whether it was a packet of pins or a yard of tape—a very paradise for haberdashers with their eternal three farthings. The man who was standing treat all round, and the more the merrier, had been a dockyard labourer in London, a grovelling grub, who at the end of the week had not twopence to spare, and probably would have been glad to accept that much charity from the hands of the kindly-hearted. In Princetown he was a lord, and just now seemed bent upon getting as drunk as one. He had struck a new lead, and on this day had washed out more than he would have received for two years' labour at home. Small wonder that his head was turned; small wonder for his belief that he was in possession of a Midas mine of wealth which would prove inexhaustible. Thus in varied form ran the story of these newly-opened goldfields with their delirious excitements and golden hopes. A new era had dawned upon mankind, and bone and muscle were the valuable commodities. So believed the miners, the kings of the land; the bush roads teemed with them, and a tramp of a hundred miles was thought nothing of. Their swags on their backs, they marched through bush and forest, and lit their camp fires at night, and sat round the blazing logs, smoking, singing, and telling bush yarns, until, healthfully tired out with their day's labour, they wrapped themselves in their blankets and slept soundly with the stars shining on them. Up they rose in the morning, as merry as Robin Hood's men, and drawing water from the creek in which they washed, made their tea and baked their "damper," then shouldered their swags again, and resumed their cheerful march. Soldiers of civilisation they, opening up a new country in which fortunes were

made and work honestly paid for. No room
for that pestilential brood, the hydra-headed
middleman, who pays the producer a shilling
for his wares, and, passing it on from hand to
hand, delivers it to the consumer at six times
its proper value. It is this multiplying process
which makes life so hard to hundreds of thousands in the over-crowded countries of the
old world.

Some passing features of the sudden crea-
tion of Princetown have been given, but one
remains to be introduced. Exactly twelve
days from the discovery of gold in the valley,
an ancient horse of lean proportions, dragging
a crazy old waggon behind it, halted in the
High Street in the early part of the day. By
the side of the tired animal was a pale-faced
man, who never once used his worn-out whip,
but gave kindly words to his steed in the
place of lashes. He was poorly dressed and
looked wan and anxious. When he halted
there descended from the waggon a woman
as pale-faced and anxious as himself and a
little girl brimming over with life and spirits.
The woman was his wife, the little girl his
daughter. The frontages to the most desirable allotments had been pegged out a long

24*

way north and south, and there were specula-
tors who had no intention of occupying these
allotments themselves, but were prepared to
sell their rights to new-comers. After a few
inquiries and some shrewd examination of the
allotments, the man bargained for one in a
suitable position, and became its owner. Then
from the waggon was taken a tent of stout
canvas, and while the old horse ate its corn
and bent its head to have its nose stroked by
the little girl, the man and woman set to work
to build their habitation. In the course of
the afternoon this was done, and then, after
an *al fresco* repast the waggon was unloaded
of its contents. This process aroused the
curiosity of the loungers in High Street,
Princetown, the goods being of an unusual
character. Mysterious looking articles were
taken out of the waggon and conveyed with
great care into the tent, and presently one
on-looker, better informed than his comrades,
cried :

" Why, it's a printing-office ! "

A printing-office it was, of the most modest
description, but still, a printing-office ; that
engine of enlightenment without which the
wheels of civilisation would cease to revolve.

The word was passed round, the news spread, and brought other contingents of spectators, and the canvas tent became a temple, and the pale-faced man a man of mark. Inside the temple the woman was arranging the type and cases, putting up without assistance two single frames and a double one; outside the man was answering, or endeavouring to answer, the eager questions asked of him, extracting at the same time, for his own behoof, such scraps of information as would prove useful to him. Pale as was his face, and anxious as was the look in his eyes, he was a man of energy and resource.

"Mates," he cried, "look out to-morrow morning for the first number of the *Princetown Argus*. Who'll subscribe?"

"I will," and "I will," answered a dozen voices, and the enterprising printer, who had staked his all on the venture, was immediately engaged in receiving subscriptions for his newspaper, and entering the names in a memorandum book. His face became flushed, the anxious look fled from his eyes; in less than half an hour he had thirty pounds in his pockets.

"Go and get me some news," he said, addressing his audience generally. "Never mind what it is, I'll put it into shape."

"William," cried the woman from the tent, "you must come and help me put up the press."

While the two were thus engaged, a good-natured fellow in the open took upon himself the task of receiving additional subscribers, and when the press was set up, and the master printer made his appearance again, a matter of twenty pounds was handed to him by his self-constituted lieutenant.

"Fifty pounds," whispered the adventurer to his wife. "A good start."

She nodded, beaming, and proceeded with her work, assisted by her husband. He had announced the initial number of the *Prince-town Argus* for the next morning, and out it would have to come. This would necessitate their stopping up all night, but what did that matter? They were establishing a property, and were already regarded as perhaps the most important arrival in the new township. In the middle of their work a visitor presented himself. The printer was spreading ink upon the ink table and getting his roller in order, when his visitor opened up a conversation.

" The *Princetown Argus*, eh ? "

" Yes."

" A good move.   The first number tomorrow morning ? "

" Yes."

" Can it be done ? "

" Oh, yes," said the printer confidently. " When I say done, done it is."

" That's your sort.   How many pages ? "

" Two.   The second number four."

" What do you ask for the whole of the front page in the first four numbers ? I've a mind to advertise."

The proposal staggered the printer, but he did not show it ; the woman pricked up her ears.

" A hundred pounds," replied the printer, amazed at his own boldness.

The visitor nodded, as if a hundred pounds for an advertisement were an every-day occurrence with him.

" With the option," he said, " of the next four numbers at the same price."

" You can have the option," said the printer, who could not yet be called a newspaper proprietor, because his journal was in embryo.

"Have you got some bold type? Big letters?"

"Yes. My plant is small at present, but I can do job printing as well as newspaper work. That's what I'm here for. I shall be getting new type sent on in a week or two."

"Show me 'John Jones' in big letters."

It was done almost instantaneously, and the visitor gazed at the name approvingly. It was his own.

"Now, underneath, 'Beehive Stores.'"

The letters were put together, and the printer said, "That will look well, right across the page."

John Jones nodded again. "Now, underneath that, 'The Beehive, The Beehive, The Only Beehive. John Jones, John Jones, The Only John Jones. Look out for the Flag, Painted by the Finest Artist of the Age.'"

"Go slow," said the printer. "All right, I'm up to you."

"'Buy Everything you Want,'" proceeded John Jones, watching the nimble fingers with admiration, "'at the only Beehive, of the only John Jones. Groceries, Provisions, Clothing of every description, Picks and Shovels, Powder and Fuse, Candles, Tubs and Dishes, Crockery, Bottled Ale and Stout, Everything of the Very Best. The highest price given for Gold. Come One, Come All. The Only Beehive. The Only John Jones. The Flag that's Braved a Thousand Years the Battle and the Breeze. Good luck to all.' There, that's the advertisement. Spread it out, you know. Here's the hundred pounds. You might give me a paragraph."

"I'll do that," said the printer. Something in this style : ' We have much pleasure in directing our readers' attention to the advertisement of our enterprising townsman, John Jones, the Beehive Stores, at whose emporium gold-diggers and others will find the finest stock of goods,' &c., &c., &c. Will that do ? "

" Capitally," said John Jones. " Put me down as a subscriber." And off went the enterprising storekeeper, satisfied with his outlay and that it would bring him a good return. Both he and William Simmons, the founder of *The Princetown Argus*, are types. It is opportunity that makes the man.

The midnight oil was burned in the new printing-office until the sun rose next morning. Not a wink of sleep did William Simmons or his wife have; she was almost as expert a compositor as her husband, and she is presented to the reader standing before her case, composing-stick in hand, picking up stamps, as a woman worthy of the highest admiration. When she paused in her work it was to have a peep at her little girl, who was sleeping soundly, and to stoop and give her darling a kiss. William Simmons was the busiest of men the whole of the time, in and out of his tent, running here and there to pick up scraps of information for paragraphs and short articles, and setting up his leading article, introducing *The Princetown Argus* to the world, literally " out of his head," for he did not write it first and put it in type afterwards, but performed the feat, of which few compositors are capable, that of making his thoughts take the place of " copy." At ten o'clock in the morning the first copy of the newspaper was produced, William Simmons being the pressman and Mrs. Simmons the roller boy. It is a curiosity in its way, and readers at the British Museum should look it up. There was a great demand for copies, and Simmons and his wife did their best to supply it, but they could not hold out longer than twelve o'clock, at which hour they shut up shop, and, throwing themselves upon some blankets on the ground, enjoyed the repose which they had so worthily earned. Before they awoke something took place which created a great stir in the township, and news of it was conveyed to the office of *The Princetown Argus*. Aroused from their sleep, the printer and his wife were up and astir again, and getting his material together, William Simmons, on the following day, issued an " extra edition " of his paper, the principal item of which is given in the next chapter.

CHAPTER VIII

"A SAD discovery" (wrote the editor and proprietor of *The Princetown Argus*) "was yesterday made on a spot some dozen miles from Princetown, which we hasten to place before our readers in the shape of an extra edition of our journal, the success of the first number of which, we are happy to say, has exceeded our most glowing anticipations. We ask the inhabitants of Princetown to accept the issue of this our first extra edition as a guarantee of the spirit with which we intend to conduct the newspaper which will represent their interests. The facts of the discovery we refer to are as follows :

"At the distance we have named from Princetown runs the Plenteous River, towards which the eyes of our enterprising miners have been already turned as the source from which, when our creeks run dry, we shall have to obtain our water supply. The party

of miners who have formed themselves into a
company for the purpose of sluicing a portion
of the ground in Fairman's Flat, deputed two
of their number, Joseph Porter and Steve
Fairfax, to make an inspection of the lay of
the land between Plenteous River and Fairman's Flat, to decide upon the feasibility of
cutting a water race, and upon the best
means of carrying out the design. The
ground they hold has been proved to be
highly auriferous, and there is no doubt that
rich washings-out will reward their enterprise.
It was not to be expected that they would
make their examination without prospecting
the ground here and there, and the reports
they have brought in seem to establish the
fact that the whole of the country between
Princetown and the Plenteous River consti-
tutes one vast goldfield. The future of our
township is assured, and within a short time
its position will be second to none in all
Australia. The report of Porter and Fairfax
is also highly favourable to the contemplated
water race, and the work will be commenced
at once. It is calculated that there are
already six thousand miners in Princetown.
We have room for five times six thousand,

and we extend the hand of welcome to our
new comrades.

"Upon the arrival of Porter and Fairfax
at the Plenteous River they naturally con-
cluded that they were the first on the ground,
no accounts of any gold workings thereabouts
having been published in any of the Australian journals. They soon discovered their
error. Work had been done on the banks of
the river, as was shown by the heaps of
tailings in different places, and on one of the
ranges sloping upwards from the banks a
shaft had been sunk. At no great distance
from the shaft a small tent was set up, and
the two men proceeded to it for the purpose
of making inquiries. Although the tent presented evidences of having been quite recently
occupied, no person was visible, and they
came to the conclusion that its owner was at
work in another direction and would return
at the close of day. Their curiosity induced
them to examine the shaft which had been
sunk on the range, and this examination led
to an important result. There was no windlass over the shaft, but a rope securely
fastened at the top hung down the mouth.
They shook the rope, and ascertained that it

hung loose. To their repeated calls down the shaft they received no reply, and they pulled up the rope. To their surprise there were not more than twelve feet of rope hanging down, whereas the stuff that had been hauled up indicated a depth of some forty or fifty feet. A closer examination of the rope showed that it had been broken at a part where it had got frayed and unable to bear a heavy weight. Being provided with a considerable length of rope the men resolved to descend the shaft and ascertain whether an accident had occurred. Having made their rope fast, Fairfax descended, and reaching the bottom was horrified to discover a man lying there senseless and apparently dead. As little time as possible was lost in getting him to the top, a work of considerable difficulty and danger, but it was accomplished safely after great labour. Then came the task of ascertaining whether the man was dead. He was not; but although he exhibited signs of life the injuries he received were of such a nature that they feared there was little hope for him. It was impossible for Fairfax and Porter to convey him to Princetown without a horse and cart, and

Fairfax hurried back to the township to obtain what was necessary, while Porter remained at the Plenteous River to nurse the injured man. He has been brought here, and is now being well looked after. The latest reports of him are more favourable, and hopes are entertained that his life may be saved. He has not yet, however, recovered consciousness, and nothing is known as to his name. Neither is anything absolutely precise known of the circumstances of the accident, except that it was caused by the breaking of the rope, a portion of which was found at the bottom of the shaft, tightly clenched in the stranger's hand.

"There is a certain element of mystery in the affair, and we shall briefly allude to one or two points which seem to have a bearing upon it.

"Fairfax and Porter, to whose timely arrival at Plenteous River the stranger undoubtedly owes his life, if it is spared, are of the opinion that there were two men working in the shaft and living together in the tent. Upon the former point they may be mistaken, for the rope was so fixed that a man working by himself could ascend and descend the shaft with comparative ease, although the labour of filling each bucket of stuff below and then ascending to the top to draw it up, would have been excessive. But upon the latter point there can be no doubt, for the reason that the tent contained two beds, both of which must have been lain upon within the last week or two. Inferring that there *were* two men working the shaft, is it possible, when the accident occurred, that the man at the top of the shaft made tracks from the place and left his mate to a cruel and lingering death? This is mere theory, and we present it for what it is worth. An opinion has been expressed that the rope has been tampered with and that it did not break from natural wear and tear. If so, it strengthens the theory we have presented. Nothing was found in the pockets of the injured man which could lead to his identity, nor was any gold found upon his person or in the tent. Thus, for the present, the affair is wrapt in mystery."

In the next week's number of the *Princetown Argus* the incident was again referred to in a leading article, in which a number of other matters found mention:

"The man who was found at the bottom of
a shaft on a range at the Plenteous River and
was brought to Princetown to have his injuries attended to, is now conscious and in a
fair way of recovery. But, whether from a
set purpose or from the circumstance that his
mental powers have been impaired from the
injuries he received, he is singularly reticent
about the affair. He has volunteered no information, and his answers to questions
addressed to him throw no light upon the
mystery. It is expected that several weeks
will elapse before he can recover his strength.
Meanwhile we have to record that gold has
been found in paying quantities in the banks
of the river and in the adjacent ranges, and
it is calculated that there are already five
hundred men at work there. Gold is also
being discovered in various parts of the
country between Princetown and the river,
and a great many claims are being profitably
worked. The rush of gold-diggers to Princetown continues, and men are pouring in every
day. Yesterday the gold escort took down
4,300 ounces ; it is expected that this quantity will be doubled next week. Our enterprising townsman, Mr. John Jones, of the

famous Beehive Stores, is having a wooden building erected in which his extensive business will in future be transacted. We direct the attention of our readers to Mr. Jones' advertisement on our front page. The enterprising proprietor of the Royal Hotel has determined to construct a movable theatre, also of wood, which will be put up every evening in the cattle sale-yards adjoining his hotel when the sales of the day are over, and taken down after every performance to allow of the sales being resumed the next morning. This is a novel idea, and will be crowned with success. A first-class company is on its way to Princetown, and it is announced that the first performance will be given in a fortnight. Fuller particulars of these matters will be found in other columns. Our readers will observe that we have doubled the size of the *Princetown Argus*, which now consists of four pages. We have ordered an entire new plant, and upon its arrival shall still further enlarge our paper. Our motto is Onward."

It will be seen from these extracts that Newman Chaytor had carried out his cruel scheme to what he believed and hoped would be the end of the comrade he had plotted

against and betrayed. But what man proposes sometimes fails in its purpose, and it
was so in this instance. The merciful arrival
of the two gold-diggers upon the scene saved
Basil's life.

This last act of Chaytor's was easily accomplished. While Basil slept he crawled to the
shaft, and by the moon's light weakened the
strands of the rope some ten feet down. Then
he crawled back to his bed, and tossed to and
fro till the dawn of day.

"We'll work the claim till the end of the
week," he said to Basil over breakfast, "and
if it turns out no better, we will try the banks
of the river again."

"Very well," said Basil. "I am truly sorry
I don't bring you better luck, but we have
something to go on with, at all events."

They walked to the shaft together, and
Basil prepared to descend. Grasping the
rope, he looked up at Chaytor, and Chaytor
smiled at him. He responded with a cheerful look, for although the hopes in which he
had indulged of returning to England with a
fortune were destroyed, he had not abandoned his wish to leave the colony. He was
sick of the life he was leading, and he yearned

for a closer human sympathy. His share of
the gold they had obtained would be close
upon five hundred pounds—that was something; it would enable him to take passage
home, to find Annette perhaps, to see and
speak with her and renew the old bond; and
if the worst happened, if he could not find
Annette, or found her only to learn that the
woman was different from the child, he could
come back to Australia and live out his life
there.

"Don't lose heart," he said to Chaytor;
"we may strike the vein again this week.
There's a bright future before you, I am
certain."

"I half believe so myself," said Chaytor;
"hoping against hope, you know." And
thought, "Will he never go down?"

Basil gave one upward look at the floating
clouds and descended. Chaytor bent over
the mouth of the shaft, looked down, and
listened.

"Is the rope firm?" Basil cried out.

"Quite firm," said Chaytor.

Then there came a terrified scream, and
the sound of a heavy body falling. Then—
silence.

Chaytor, with white face and lips tightly set, still bent over the mouth of the shaft, still looked down the dark depths, still listened. Not a sound—not even a groan.

"It is done," he muttered.

He pulled up the severed rope, and thought that it might have happened without his intervention. He had read of a parallel instance, and of the death of a miner in consequence.

"It was an accident," he said, "as this is. The rope would have given way without my touching it. Such things occur all over the world. Look at the colliery accidents at home—hundreds of men are killed in them, here there is only one."

These thoughts were not prompted by compunction ; he simply desired to shift the responsibility from his own shoulders. It was a miserable subterfuge, and did not succeed. In the first flush of his crime its shadow haunted him.

He let the rope fall from his hand down the shaft. " I could not go to him," he said, " if I wanted. How quiet he is !"

A mad impulse seized him.

" Basil ! Basil ! " he cried in his loudest

tone ; and as no reply reached him, he said,
looking around, " Well, then, is it my fault
that he does not answer me ? "

He paced to and fro, a dozen steps this
way, a dozen that, counting his steps. Fifty
times at least he did this, always with the
intention of going to the tent or the river,
and always being drawn back to the mouth
of the shaft, over which he hung and lingered.
It possessed a horrible fascination for him.

" I *will* go this time," he said, but he could
not. He remained an hour—the longest hour
in his life. At length he went down to the
river, and as he gazed upon it thought, " Men
die by drowning. What does it matter the
kind of death ? Death is death : it is always
the same."

The interminable hours lagged on till night
came. He sat in the tent weighing the gold
and getting ready for flight. Once in Sydney
he would take the first ship for England.
The flickering candle cast monstrous shadows
upon the walls and ceiling, and in his
nervous state he shrank shudderingly from
them, and strove to ward them off, as though
they were living forms hovering about him
with fell intent. The silence appalled him ;

he would have given gold for the piping of a little bird.

Thus passed the miserable night, and in the morning he visited the shaft again. The same awful stillness reigned.

"It is all over," he said. "Newman Chaytor is dead ; I, Basil Whittingham, live. No man will ever know. Now for England!"

CHAPTER IX.

OCCASIONALLY in a man's life comes a pause: as between the acts of a drama action slumbers awhile—only that the march through life's season never halts. The pulse of time throbs silently and steadily until the natural span is reached, or is earlier snapped, and the bridge between mortality and immortality is crossed. Meanwhile the man grows older —that is all. For him upon the tree of experience there is neither blossom nor bloom ; bare branches spread out, naked of hope, and he gazes upon them in dumb wonderment or despair. The hum of woodland life, the panorama of wondrous colour, the unceasing growth of life out of death, the warlike sun, the breath of peace in moon and stars, the eternal pæan that all nature sings, bear no message to his soul. He walks, he eats, he sleeps, and waits unconsciously for the divine touch that shall arouse him from his trance.

Something of this kind occurred to Basil. Recovering from the physical injuries he had sustained, he sank into an apathetic state which, but for some powerful incentive, might have been morally fatal. Friends he had none, or the effort might have been made ; so for a year after Newman Chaytor had left Australia he plodded aimlessly on, working for wages which kept him in food, and desiring nothing more. Upon the subject of his mate's desertion he preserved silence, as indeed he did upon most other subjects, but it might reasonably have been expected that upon this theme in which he was directly interested he would have been willing to open his mind. It was not so. To questions addressed to him he returned brief and unsatisfactory answers, and after a time nothing further was asked of him. Curiosity died out ; if he chose to keep himself aloof it was his business, and in the new world as in the old, every man's affairs were sufficient to occupy him without troubling himself about strangers. Thus it would appear that the scheme upon which Newman Chaytor had bent all his energies was destined to be in every way successful.

With respect to the desertion and the disappearance of the gold, an equal share of which was rightfully and lawfully his, Basil had arrived at a definite conclusion. He entertained no doubt that the rope had broken naturally; suspicion of foul play did not cross his mind. He argued that Chaytor, believing him to be dead, had taken the gold and left the claim they had been working in disgust. "He made no secret," thought Basil, "that he was sick of the life we were leading. To have gone away and left my share of the gold behind him—I being, as he supposed, dead—would have been an act of folly. I do not blame him; good luck go with him. He stuck to me to the last, and proved himself my friend when most I needed one. Let my life go on as it will; I will think nothing and say nothing to his injury." A vindictive man would have argued otherwise, would have thought that it was at least a comrade's duty, before he left the spot, to convince himself by ocular proof that the fall was fatal. But Basil was not vindictive; he believed he had the best of reasons to be grateful to Chaytor, and if the gold his mate had taken was any repayment for services rendered in the past, he was welcome to it. The strong moral principle in Basil's nature kept him from yielding to temptations against which not all men struggle successfully when misfortune persistently dogs them. He led an honest life of toil, without ambition to lift himself to a higher level. But happily an awakening was in store for him, and it came through the sweetest and most humanising of influences.

Princetown throve apace ; its promise was fulfilled, and twenty thousand men found prosperous lodgment therein. The majority delved, the minority traded, most of them throve. To be sure some were unfortunate, and some idled and dissipated, but this must always be expected. New leads were dis· covered, quartz reefs were opened, crushing machines were put up, streets were formed, a fire brigade was established, a benevolent institution and a lunatic asylum were founded. Not even a mushroom town in these new countries can exist without something in the shape of a municipal council, and one was formed in Princetown, over the elections for which there was prodigious excitement. Churches and chapels, even a synagogue,

were erected by voluntary contributions, and
there were churchyards in which already
wanderers found rest. All the important
buildings were now of wood, and there was a
talk of stone, the primal honour of erecting
which was presently to fall to John Jones, the
enterprising proprietor of the Only Beehive.
The *Princetown Argus* shared in the general
prosperity. First a weekly then a bi-weekly,
then a tri-weekly, finally a daily. First, two
pages, the size of the *Globe*, then four pages
ditto, finally four pages, the size of the *Times*.
Not a bad sample of enterprise this. The
Saturday edition was eight pages, to serve the
purpose of a weekly as well as a daily, and in
it was published a novel, " to be continued in
our next," which the editor took from a
London monthly magazine, and for which, in
the innocence of his heart, he paid nothing.
Of course there was an opposition journal,
but the *Princetown Argus* had taken the lead,
and kept it in the face of all newcomers.
The shrewd editor and proprietor did one
piece of business with a more than usually
obstinate rival which deserves to be recorded.
He bought up an opposition paper, the
Princetown Herald, whose politics were the

reverse of those he advocated, and for a considerable time he ran the two papers on their original lines, each attacking the other's principles and policy with fierce zest and vigour. Thus he occupied both fields of public opinion, and threw sops to all who took an interest in local and colonial politics. And here a word in the shape of information which will surprise many readers. England is overrun with newspapers; the United States is more than overrun, having nearly three to our one; but in journalistic enterprise Australasia beats the record, having, in proportion to population, more newspapers than any other country in the world. An astonishing fact.

Two circumstances must be mentioned which bear upon our story. The first is that Basil's surname was not known; he called himself Basil, and was so called. The second is that in the column of the *Princetown Argus* in which births, marriages, and deaths were advertised, there was recorded the birth and death of a baby, the child of the editor and his wife, born one day and dying the next. This was the first birth and burial in Princetown. The child left to them, the little girl of whom we have already spoken, whose name was Edith, took the loss of her baby sister much to heart, and never a week passed that she did not visit the churchyard and sit by the tiny grave.

At the end of twelvemonths or so there came to Princetown a preacher of extraordinary power. He was rough, he was uncultivated, he had not been educated for the pulpit, but he could stir the masses and wake up sleeping souls. He had a marvellous magnetism and tremendous earnestness, which silenced the scoffer and made the sinner tremble ; the consequence was that sinners and scoffers went to hear him, and some few were made better by his denunciations. There are souls which can be reached only through fear. Happily there are more which can be reached through love.

Amongst those who were drawn to listen to the preacher was Basil, and being once present he did not miss a service. One Sabbath the preacher took sluggishness for his theme, which he denounced, in its physical and moral attributes, as a sin, the consequences of which were not to be avoided. Men were sent into the world to work, to fulfil duties, and to seek both assiduously. It was not only sinful, it was cowardly, to put on the armour of indolence and indifference, and to so intrench oneself was destructive of the highest qualities of humanity, the exercise of which lifted men above the level of the beasts of the field. To say, because one is unfortunate, " Oh, what is the use of striving ? " tends to rob life of nobility and heroism. To fight the battle manfully to the last, to keep one's heart open to humanising influences, however poor the return which proffered love and sympathy and charity may meet with, is the work of a man and brings its reward. He has striven, he has proved himself, he has established his claim to the higher life. To live only for the day, to be indifferent to the morrow, is a quality by which animals without reason are distinguished, and to share with them in this respect is a cowardly and sinful degradation. " If " (said the preacher) " there are any here who have fallen so low, I say to them, Arouse yourselves ; take down the shutters which darken heart and soul ; admit the light which purifies and sweetens. Be men, not brutes."

This was the sum of his sermon. Few

understood it, but they did not perhaps value
it the less highly on that account. To Basil
it came as a reproach; he quivered under
the strokes and left the place of worship with
a beating heart, with tumultuous thoughts in
his mind. Scarcely noting whither he was
going he walked towards the churchyard, and
there in the distance, sitting by a grave, he
saw a child. It was Edith sitting by the
grave of her baby sister.

The scene, the attitude, brought Annette's
form to his mind. So used she to sit by her
mother's grave on the plantation, and he had
accompanied her and sat by her side. He
looked about for flowers; there were none
near; but when he approached Edith he saw
that she had some in her lap, and was
weaving them into a garland, as Annette had
done in a time really not so very long ago,
but which seemed to belong to another life.
She looked up at him, and the tenderness of
her gaze touched him deeply; instantly on
her countenance was reflected the sad wistful-
ness which dwelt on his. Children are
peculiarly receptive; they meet your smiles
with smiles, your sadness with sadness. Edith
just shifted her little body, conveying in the

slight movement an invitation to Basil to sit beside her. He instantly took his place close to her, and they fell naturally into conversation."

" What is your name, little one ? "

" Edith. Tell me yours. I like you."

" My name is Basil."

" I like that, too. Here is a flower for you."

" Where did you gather, them, Edith."

" We have a garden. Father says it puts him in mind of home."

" Who is your father ? "

" Don't you know ? Everybody else does. He's the editor of the *Princetown Argus*. You know that, don't you ? "

" Yes. And you have a mother ? "

" Oh, yes. She is very clever." Basil nodded. " Father says she is the cleverest woman in the whole world. She can make clothes, she can cook, she knows all about flowers, she can write paragraphs for the paper, and when they are written she can print them."

" That is a great deal for your mother to do. Does she really help to print the newspaper ? "

"Not now. She did when we first came here. But father has a great many gentlemen printers in the office, and they do all that. These are English flowers. The seeds come all the way from England where I was born; but I don't remember it because I was only a little baby when we came over in a great big ship. I don't remember the ship either, but I know all about it because mother has told me about the great storm, and how we were nearly wrecked, and how the ship was battered to pieces almost."

"The English flowers put your father in mind of home. That is England?"

"Yes, that is England. When we're very rich we're going back there. Do you know where it is?"

"I come from England."

"That is nice. Like us. Are you going back?"

"I cannot say."

"Why? Because you don't know?"

"That is the reason, perhaps."

"You see," said Edith, arranging some flowers on the grave in the shape of a cross, "there are so many people there we love. Two grandfathers, two grandmothers, and

such a lot of cousins I've never seen.
England must be very, very beautiful.
Father and mother call it home, and when I
write I always say, 'We are coming home
one day.' We're going to have a fig-tree;
father says we shall sit under it." Basil
smiled. "I like you to smile; you don't
look so unhappy then. What makes you
unhappy? You mustn't be. You must go
home with us and see the people you love."

"Suppose there are none, little Edith."

She gazed at him solemnly. "Not even an
angel?" she asked.

"An angel!" he exclaimed, somewhat
startled.

"Yes, an angel. One was here once."
She had completed the cross of flowers, and
she pointed to the grave. "Only for a little
while, and when we go home she is coming
with us. She came from heaven to us just
for one night only; I was asleep and didn't
see her; I was so sorry. Then they brought
her here, and she flew straight up to heaven.
I can't go up there to give her the English
flowers, so I lay them here where she can see
them, and when I come again and the flowers
are gone I know that she has taken them

away and put them in a jug of water—up
there.   Mother says flowers never die in
heaven, so baby sister must have a lot.   I
dream of her sometimes ; I wish you could
see her as I do.   There's a picture of a baby
angel over my bed, and she is just like that.
Such beautiful large grey eyes—my eyes are
grey—and shining wings.   We love each
other dearly."

"I hope that will always be, little Edith."

"Oh, it will be.   When you love once you
love always ; that is what mother says, and
she never says anything wrong.   I wish you
had an angel."

"I had one once."

"Why, then you have one now.   Once
means always.   Was she a little girl?"

"Yes."

"Like our angel.   I am glad.   Now you
must come and see mother and father."   She
rose and took his hand.

"They do not know me, Edith."

"But *I* know you, and you know me.   You
must come."

"Yes, I will come.   May I take one flower
from your cross?"

"Yes."

He selected one and kissed it, and they walked together side by side. The preacher had said, "Take down the shutters which darken heart and soul; admit the light which purifies and sweetens." It was done, and the light was shining in Basil's heart. He clung to the little hand which was clasped in his. In that good hour it was indeed a Divine link which re-united him once more to what was best and noblest. The shadows were dying away. Dark days were before him, strange experiences were to be his, but in the darkest day of the future a star was always to shine. "Annette, Annette, Annette," he whispered. "I will make an endeavour to see you. I will never again lose faith. A weight has gone from my heart."

"Let me kiss the flower where you kissed it," said Edith.

He put it to her lips, and she kissed it, and raised her face innocently. He stooped and kissed her lips.

"I think," said Edith, contemplatively, "I like you better than any one else except mother and father and baby angel."

The office of the *Princetown Argus* was now an extensive building, all on one floor;

architects had not yet reached higher flights. The door from the street opened midway between two rooms, the one to the right being that in which advertisements and orders for subscriptions were taken, the one to the left being used for book-keeper, editor, and reporters indiscriminately. The reporting staff did a great part of their work standing; there were only a desk and a stool for the book-keeper, who assisted in the reading of proofs, and a table and two chairs for the accommodation of the editor and sub-editor. Adjoining these two rooms in the rear was the composing-room of the newspaper, in the rear of that the jobbing-room, in the rear of that the press room. The living apartments of the editor and his little family were quite at the end of the building, and were really commodious—sitting-room, kitchen, and two sleeping-rooms, one for little Edith, the other for her parents. In the sitting-room there was a piano upon which every member of the family could play with one finger, there were framed chromos on the walls, and sufficient accommodation in the shape of chairs and tables. The mantelpiece was embellished with an extensive array of photographs of grandfathers, grandmothers, uncles, aunts, and cousins; and the floor was covered with red baize. Taking it altogether it was an elegant abode for a new goldfield, and Edith's garden, upon which the window of her bed-room looked out, imparted to it an air of refinement and sweetness exceedingly pleasant to contemplate. When Edith, still holding Basil's hand, passed through the business rooms and entered the sitting-room, the happy editor and proprietor was alone, his wife being busy in the kitchen getting dinner ready. Domestic servants were the rarest of birds in Princetown; indeed there were none in the private establishments, for as soon as a girl or a woman made her appearance in the township there was a "rush" for her, and before she had been there a week she had at least a dozen offers of marriage. A single woman was worth her weight in gold— Princetown was a veritable paradise for spinsters of any age, from fifteen to fifty. Small wonder that they turned up their noses at domestic service, when by merely crooking their little finger they could become their own mistress, picking and choosing from a host of amorous gold diggers. Free and easy was the wedding ; the eating and drinking, the popping of corks, the drive through the principal streets, the indiscriminate invitations to all, the dancing at night, with more popping of corks and the cracking of revolvers in the open air to proclaim to the world that an " event " of supreme importance was being celebrated—all tended to show the value of woman as a marketable commodity. Two or three miles away, in a gully or upon a hill, was the canvas tent to which the bridegroom bore his bride an hour or two this or that side of midnight, literally bore her often because of the open shafts which dotted the road ; and there the married life commenced. It is a lame metaphor to say that woman ruled the roast ; she ruled everything, and was bowed down to and worshipped as woman never was before in the history of the world.

The editor looked up as his little daughter and Basil entered, and Edith immediately took upon herself the office of mistress of the ceremonies.

"This is Basil, father." The editor nodded. "He is going to spend the whole day with us."

"He is welcome," said the editor, who knew Basil by sight.

Basil smilingly explained that little Edith had taken entire possession, and was responsible for his intrusion.

"But you are not intruding," said the editor. "We shall be very pleased of your company. Our hive is ruled by a positive Queen Bee, and there she stands"—with an affectionate look at his daughter, who accepted her title with amusing gravity—"so that we cannot exactly help ourselves."

His tone was exceedingly cordial, and Basil, being heartily welcomed by Edith's mother, soon made himself at home. The young man's manners were very winning and afforded pleasure to Edith's parents, who had not, at least on the goldfields, met with a guest of so much culture and refinement. Regarding Basil as her special property, Edith pretty well monopolised his attention in the intervals between meals, but sufficient of Basil's character was revealed to the editor to set him thinking. He saw that he was entertaining a gentlemen and a man of attainments, and he felt how valuable such an assistant would be on the editorial staff of his newspaper. The journalists in his employ had sprung out of the rough elements of colonial life, and although they were fairly capable men, they lacked the polish which Basil possessed. The result of his reflections was that before the day was out he made Basil a business proposition.

"It occurs to me," said the shrewd fellow, "that you are not exactly cut out for a digger's life."

"I am afraid you are right," said Basil, with a smile in which a touch of sadness might be detected.

"Why not try something else?" asked the editor.

"It is difficult to know what," replied Basil; "there are so few things for which I am fitted."

"There is one in which you would make your mark."

"May I know what it is? I may differ from you; but it would be a pleasant hearing."

"Sub-editor of the *Princetown Argus*, for instance," suggested the editor, coming straight to the point. He was not the kind of man to take two bites at a cherry.

Basil looked him in the face; the proposition startled and gratified him. "You rush at a conclusion somewhat hastily," he said.

"Not at all. I know what I am talking about. You are cut out for just that position."

"I have never done anything in the literary way."

"I'll take the risk," said the editor. "A man may go floundering about all his life without falling into his proper groove. You are not bound to any other engagement in Princetown?"

"To none. I am quite free."

"And you can commence at once?"

"If you are serious."

"I was never more so. It might be agreeable to you to take up your quarters with us. In two days I will have a sleeping apartment built for you, adjoining our little bit of garden. You are a sociable man and a gentleman, and we should be glad to have you at our table. From your conversation I should say you have had a classical education. Am I right?"

"Quite right; but I am not a very bright scholar. You must not expect great things."

" I expect what you are able to supply ;
you haven't half enough confidence in your
self. Why, if I had your advantages—but
never mind, I haven't done badly with my small
stock of brains. We'll wake them up." He
rubbed his hands. " You will be a bit strange
at first, but I'll put you in the way of things.
I look upon it as settled."

" Would it not be prudent," said Basil,
" for you to take a little time for consideration ? "

" Not an hour ; not a minute. Strike
while the iron's hot. My dear sir, this is a
go-ahead country. Shake hands on the
bargain."

They shook hands upon it, and immediately
afterwards the editor regarded Basil with a
thoughtful air, and said :

" You puzzle me, you do not ask anything
about terms."

" I am content to leave them to you.
Wait till you see whether I am worth anything."

" No, the risk is mine, as I have said. Will
six pounds a week and board and lodging suit
you ? "

" It is too much."

"You will be satisfied with it for the first month?"

"More than satisfied."

"It is arranged, then. If we continue together you shall have an advance at the end of the month, and I shall bind you down not to leave me without a month's notice.

"On my part, I will be so bound. You are free to discharge me without notice."

"It shall be the same for both of us. As you are to commence to-morrow you might think of a subject for a 'leader' in Tuesday's paper. By Wednesday your bedroom will be ready, and you can live with us as long as you are on the staff. We shall have reason to congratulate ourselves on the arrangement we have made."

CHAPTER X.

CERTAINLY neither Basil nor his employer had
reason to be otherwise. It led to important
results in Basil's career, and in years to come
he often thought of the child, the chance
meeting with whom in the churchyard conducted him, by both straight and devious
paths, to a goal which he had not dared to
hope he would ever reach. Between him and
Edith loving links were soon firmly forged
which time was never to sever. This sweet
and human bond was of inestimable value to
Basil; it raised him from the slough of
despond into which he had sunk; the hand of
a little child lifted him to a man's height.
He was profoundly grateful; he had now a
happy home, he had congenial work to do.
The doubts he had entertained of his fitness
for the position were dispelled in a very short
time. He threw himself with ardour and
animation into his new duties, which he per-

formed in a manner that more than justified
the confidence reposed in him. Nominally sub-
editor, but really editor of the paper, he infused into its columns a spirit of intelligence
which made it more popular than ever. It was
talked of as an example of what a newspaper
should be, and Basil's opinions upon colonial
matters were quoted in the more influential
journals in the colonies as those of a man of
far-seeing judgment. A classical allusion now
and then added to the value of Basil's
writings, and all Princetown was proud of
him because of the vicarious distinction
conferred, through him, upon its inhabitants.
"A clever fellow that," said John Jones, of
the Only Beehive, appreciating Basil the more
because of his own utter ignorance of the
classics. There was a talk of Basil's representing the division in the Legislative
Assembly, but he promptly set that aside
by emphatically declaring that he had no
desire for public life or parliamentary
honours. Thus six months passed by, when
a revelation was made to him which caused
him to carry out a resolve deplored by all
Princetown.

The official quarters of the township, where

public business was transacted, was known as
the Government Camp. In this camp, which
was laid out upon the slope of a hill, were
situated the Magistrate's Court, the buildings
in which the mounted troopers lodged, where
the gold escort was made up, where miners'
disputes were adjusted, and where miners
paid their yearly sovereign for miners' rights,
which gave lawful sanction to their delving
for the precious metal and appropriating the
treasure they extracted from the soil.
There were swells in the Government Camp,
members of good families in the old country,
for whom something in the shape of official
employment had to be found. It is
pleasant to be able to record that there
were few sinecures among these employ-
ments, most of the holders having to do
something in the shape of work for their
salaries. It was when Basil had served on
the staff of the *Princetown Argus* for a space
of six months, and had saved during that
period a matter of two hundred pounds, that
a new Goldfields' Warden made his appearance at the Government Camp. The name of
this gentleman was Majoribanks, and when
we presently part with him he will play no

further part in our story ; but it will be seen that the small *rôle* he fills in it is sufficiently pregnant.

Mr. Majoribanks was " a new chum " in the colony. Arriving in the capital with high credentials, the influence of his connections provided him almost immediately with a berth to which a good salary, with pickings, was attached. The position of Goldfields' Warden on Princetown was vacant, and he was appointed to it. His special fitness for the office need not here be discussed. Many members of good families in England, whose wild ways rendered desirable their removal to another sphere, developed faculties in Australia which elevated them into respectable members of society, which they certainly would not have been had they remained in the old world, surrounded by temptations. Mr. Majoribanks was not a bad fellow at bottom, and it was a fortunate day for him and his family when they exchanged farewell greetings.

There were not many gentlemen—in Mr. Majoribanks' understanding of the term—in Princetown, and when the new Goldfields' Warden came in contact with Basil, he recognised the superior metal in the hero of our story. The casual acquaintance they formed ripened into intimacy, and they met often in Mr. Majoribanks' quarters and passed many a pleasant hour together.

"Come and have a smoke this evening," said Mr. Majoribanks to Basil one Saturday afternoon.

Saturday was the only day in the week which Basil could call his own, and he was glad of the invitation and accepted it. Mr. Majoribanks knew Basil only, as others knew him, by the name of Basil, and had not taken the trouble to inquire whether it was a surname. So the two gentleman sat in Mr. Majoribanks' snug quarters on this particular Saturday, and discussed a dainty little meal, cooked in capital style by the Goldfields' Warden's Chinese cook. The meal finished, they adjourned to the verandah, and lit their cigars.

They had much in common; they had travelled over familiar country in Europe, and they compared notes, recalling experiences of old times which, in their likeness to each other, drew them closer together.

"Upon my soul," remarked Mr. Majori-

27*

banks, " it is an exceedingly pleasant thing to find one's self in the company of a gentle-man. It makes banishment endurable. Do you ever think of returning to England ? "

" One day, perhaps," replied Basil.

" I hope we shall meet there, said Mr. Majoribanks. " Is it allowable to ask what brought you out to the goldfields ? "

" I lost my fortune," said Basil, " and not knowing what to turn my hand to came to Australia to make another."

" Is it again allowable to ask whether you have succeeded ? "

" I have not succeeded."

" If you had been a bricklayer or a navvy in England you might tell a different tale."

" It is not unlikely."

" A gentleman stands but little chance here," observed Mr. Majoribanks. " We are treated in the colonies to a complete reversal of the proper order of things. I suppose in the course of time Australia will cut itself away from the old country and become a republic."

" It is certainly on the cards, but it will be a long time before that occurs ; there are so many different interests, you see."

"A jumble of odd elements," said Mr. Majoribanks.

"When there is a real Australian population," said Basil, "men and woman born and living here, with no reminiscences of what is now called 'home,' then the movement of absolute self-government will take serious form."

"Ah, well, I don't believe in the self-made man. I stick to the old order."

"Individual opinion will not change the current of natural changes. It is not to be expected that this vast continent will be for ever satisfied to remain a dependency of a kingdom so many thousands of miles away. The talk about federation may satisfy for a time, but it is merely a sop in the pan. By-and-by will come the larger question of a nation with an autonomous constitution like the United States. Children cut themselves from their mother's apron strings : so it will be with these colonies."

"You have made a study of such matters."

"To some extent. My position on our local paper has sent me in that direction."

"You like your position ?"

"Tolerably well. I cannot say I am wedded to it, but I must not be ungrateful."

Then the conversation drifted into chanels more personal. Mr. Majoribanks launched into a recital of certain experiences in England and the Continent, and mourned the break in a career more congenial to him than that of Goldfields' Warden in Princetown, which he declared to be confoundedly dull and uninteresting. He missed his theatres, his clubs, his race meetings, his fashionable society, and many a sigh escaped him as he dwelt upon these fascinating themes. Then occurred a pause, and some sudden reminiscence, as yet untouched, caused him to regard his companion with more than ordinary curiosity.

"An odd idea strikes me," he said. "Have you a twin brother?"

"No," replied Basil, smiling. "What makes you ask?"

"No, of course that is not likely," said Mr. Majoribanks. "If you had a twin brother his name would not be Basil. It is singular for all that. But it is a most extraordinary likeness. A cousin of yours, perhaps?"

"I haven't the slightest idea of your meaning. I have no cousins that I am aware of."

"It has only just struck me. As I looked at you a moment ago I saw the wonderful resemblance between you and a man I met in Paris. Basil is not a very common name."

"Not very. Had the gentleman you met in Paris another tacked to it?"

"Oh, yes," said Mr. Majoribanks. "Whittingham."

"Whittingham!" exclaimed Basil, greatly startled.

"Basil Whittingham—that is the gentleman's full name; and, by the way, I was told, I remember, that he had been in Australia, gold-digging. It is a curious story —but you seem excited."

"With good cause," said Basil. "My name is Basil Whittingham."

"You don't say so?"

"It is a fact."

"Well, that makes it all the stranger."

Basil rose and paced the verandah in uncontrollable excitement. The full significance of this extraordinary revelation did not immediately dawn upon him, and at present he did not connect Newman Chaytor with it. Out of the chaos of thought which stirred his mind he evoked nothing intelligible. Mr.

Majoribanks' eyes followed him as he paced
to and fro, and fixed themselves frankly upon
him when he paused and faced him.

"Were you aware that my name is Whittingham?" asked Basil.

"Upon my honour, no," replied Mr. Majoribanks.

"There is some mystery here," said Basil,
mastering his excitement, "which it seems
imperative should be solved.   As you remarked, Basil is not a common name; neither
is Whittingham ; and that the two should be
associated in the person of a man who bears
so wonderful a resemblance to me that you
would have taken us to be twin brothers,
makes it all the more mysterious and inex-
plicable.   You are not joking with me?"

"As I am a gentleman, I have told you
nothing but the truth.   There are such things
as coincidences, you know."

"Yes ; but if this is one, it is the strangest
I have ever heard of."

"It has all the appearance of it," said Mr.
Majoribanks, thoughtfully.

"Within my knowledge there are only two
men bearing the name of Whittingham—one,
myself, the other an uncle in England, with

whom, unfortunately, I had some differences of opinion."

"Ah," said Mr. Majoribanks, "the coincidences continue. The gentleman I refer to had an uncle of the name of Whittingham, with whom he also had some differences of opinion."

"*Had* an uncle?"

"Who is dead," said Mr. Majoribanks.

"My uncle was a gentleman of fortune."

"So was his."

"I was to have been his heir. I displeased him, and he disinherited me. That was really the reason why I left England for Australia."

Mr. Majoribanks fell back in his chair, and said, "You take my breath away."

"Why?"

"Why? Because that is the sum total of the story which I said just now was so curious. Mr. Whittingham, there must be something more than coincidence in all this."

"Oblige me a moment. Let me think."

He turned his back upon Mr. Majoribanks, and steadied himself. By a determined effort he subdued the chaos of thought by which he was agitated. The form of Newman

Chaytor rose before him. Was it possible that this man, in whom he had placed implicit trust, who knew the whole story of his life, who had deserted him and left him for dead without taking the trouble to assure himself that his fall down the shaft was fatal —was it possible that this man had played him false? It seemed scarcely credible, but what other construction was to be placed upon the story which Mr. Majoribanks had revealed to him. He paused again before his companion, and said in his most earnest tone:

"Mr. Majoribanks, a vital issue hangs upon the information you have given me. I am sure you will not trifle with me. You are a gentleman, and your word is not to be doubted. Were you intimately acquainted with this double, who bears my name, who so strangely resembles me, and whose story is so similar to my own?"

"There was no intimacy whatever," said Mr. Majoribanks. "I saw him once, and once only, in Paris, and we passed an evening together. When I parted from him—a party of us went to the Comédie Française that night to see Bernhardt—I saw him no more.

The way of it was this. It being resolved in solemn family council that I was to retrieve my battered fortunes in this Sahara, I paid a last visit to dear delightful Paris to bid it a long adieu. A friend accompanied me, and a friend of his to whom he was under obligations—to speak plainly, a money-lender—happening to be in Paris at the same time, we chummed together. We dined at the Grand, and there, at another table, sat your prototype. Our money-lending friend, who knows everything and everybody, pointed him out to us, and told us his story. His name was Basil Whittingham; he had been in Australia, gold-digging; he had a wealthy uncle of the same surname whom he had offended, and who had driven him out of his native land, with an intimation that he was to consider himself disinherited. Upon his deathbed, however, the old gentleman's hard heart softened, and he made a will by which the discarded nephew was restored to his good graces, and became heir to all he possessed. The fortune which fell to your lucky double was not in land and houses; it was in something better, hard cash, and it amounted, so far as I can recollect, to not less than between fifty and sixty thousand pounds. Whereupon the lucky heir winged his way homeward, by which time his uncle had joined the majority, and took possession of his windfall. Our money-lending friend had some slight acquaintance with the heir, and we were introduced. It was a night I had occasion to remember, quite apart from any connection you may have with the story. Do you adhere to it that it resembles yours?"

"Up to the day upon which I left England it agrees with it entirely. As to what subsequently occurred I knew nothing until this moment."

"Well, all that I can say—without understanding in the least, mind you, how it could have come about—is, that I would look into it, if I were in your place."

"It shall be looked into. Do you remember if the uncle's Christian name was mentioned?"

"I cannot quite say. Refresh my memory; it may have been."

"Bartholomew."

"Upon my word, now you mention it, I think Bartholomew was mentioned. Another uncommon name."

"You have occasion to remember that night, you said, apart from me. May I inquire in what way?"

"Well, when we left the theatre, we adjourned to a private room in the Grand, and there we had a little flutter. Baccarat was the game, and I was cleaned out. Upon my honour, I think I was the most unfortunate beggar under the sun. I give you my word that I hadn't enough left to pay my hotel bill, which was the last legacy I left my honoured father."

"Your money-lending friend won ‧the money, I suppose?"

"He won a bit, but the spoil fell principally to an elderly gentleman of the name of —of—of—now what *was* the fellow's name? It wasn't English, nor was he an Englishman. Ah. I have it. Bidaud—yes, Bidaud."

Basil's face turned white; there was no longer room for doubt that foul treachery had been done. It was Newman Chaytor who had plotted and planned for his destruction. This he might have borne, and the white heat of his anger might have grown cold with time. But Anthony Bidaud's introduction into the bad scheme included also

Annette, a possible victim in the treachery. That she should become the prey of these villains, and that he should allow her life to be ruined, her happiness to be blasted, without an effort to save her, was not to be thought of. The scales fell from his eyes, and he saw Newman Chaytor in his true light. By what crooked paths the end had been reached he could not, in the excitement of the moment, determine. That would have to be thought out presently; meanwhile his resolution was taken. To remain inactive would be the work of a coward.

"You know the name of Bidaud," said Mr. Majoribanks.

"I know it well," said Basil. "Did this M. Bidaud accompany you to the theatre on that night?"

"He did."

"Alone?"

"Alone."

"He and this namesake of mine were companions, I take it."

"Something more than companions, to all appearances. Close friends rather."

"Did they appear to be on good terms with each other?"

" On the best of terms."

" I hope," said Basil, " you will excuse me for questioning you so closely, but this is a matter that very deeply affects me."

" My dear fellow," said Mr. Majoribanks, " you are heartily welcome to every scrap of information I can give that will throw light upon this most mysterious piece of business. It is altogether the strangest thing I ever heard. I'll not ask you who the other fellow is, but I have a faint idea that he must be the most unmitigated scoundrel on the face of the earth. Tell me as much or as little as you please, and in the meantime fire away."

" My namesake was dining at the Grand Hotel when you first saw him? Was M. Bidaud in his company ? "

" He was ; they were dining together at a separate table."

" Were any ladies with them ? "

" I'll not pledge myself. So far as I can recollect, there was no one else at the table."

" Did you hear talk of any ladies of their acquaintance ? "

" I think not. Stop, though. I fancy there was an allusion to a pretty niece."

"Annette lives," thought Basil, and said aloud, "An allusion made by M. Bidaud to my namesake?"

"Yes, I think so."

"Who suggested the adjournment to a private room after the theatre?"

"The invitation was given by M. Bidaud, and we accepted it. I was always ready for that kind of thing—too ready, my people say. So off we went, and played till daylight, with the aforesaid result."

"Were M. Bidaud and my namesake living permanently in Paris?"

"I fancy not; something was said of their travelling about for pleasure."

"One more question," said Basil, "and I have done. There was an allusion to a pretty niece. Are you aware whether the young lady was travelling with her uncle?"

"I am not, and I do not remember what the allusion was. I think I have completely emptied my budget."

"I thank you sincerely; you have rendered me an inestimable service. I have no wish to have my affairs talked about, and you will add to the obligation if you will consider this conversation confidential."

" Certainly, my dear fellow, as you desire it.
It is entirely between ourselves."

They parted shortly afterwards, and Basil,
plunged in thought, returned to the township. The first step he took was to consult
the file of the *Princetown Argus* for a record
of the accident in which he had so nearly lost
his life. He had heard that its earliest numbers contained accounts of his discovery and
rescue, but he had not hitherto had the curiosity to hunt them up and read them. It was
now imperative that he should make himself
acquainted with every particular of the affair.
He found without difficulty what he sought,
and as he read through the reports of his
condition which were published from day
to day he dwelt upon portions which a year
ago he would have considered monstrous
inventions or exaggerations. Thus : " There
is a certain element of mystery in the affair,
and we shall briefly allude to one or two
points which seem to have a bearing upon
it." Again: " Inferring that there were two
men working the shaft, is it possible, when
the accident occurred, that the man at the
top of the shaft made tracks from the place
and left his mate to a cruel and lingering

death?" The inference here sought to be established was not to be mistaken—to wit, that Newman Chaytor had purposely left him to a cruel and lingering death. And still more significant: "An opinion has been expressed that the rope has been tampered with, and that it did not break from natural wear and tear." Given that the peril into which he had been plunged was the result of design, there was more than a seeming confirmation of the opinion that the rope had been tampered with. Basil, being now engaged upon a full consideration of the circumstances, remembered that the rope to all appearance was perfectly sound. That being so, it was Chaytor's deliberate intention to murder him by weakening the strands. When suspicion enters the mind of a man who has trusted and been deceived, it is hard to dislodge it; small incidents and spoken words to which no importance was attached at the time they were uttered, present themselves and gather force until they assume a dark significance. When Basil laid aside the file of newspapers he had arrived at the conclusion that Chaytor had deliberately schemed for the fatal end which had been averted by

the merest accident. Old Corrie's warnings
and distrust of Chaytor came to his mind.
" Corrie was right," thought Basil ; " he read
this man better than I did."

But clear as Chaytor's villany had appeared
to be, there was much that Basil was unable
to comprehend. In what way had Chaytor
discovered that Basil's uncle had repented of
his determination to disinherit his nephew ?
How and by what means had it come to the
villain's knowledge ? Upon these and other
matters Basil had yet to be enlightened.

He continued his mental search. Chaytor,
returning to England, had succeeded in obtaining possession of his inheritance ; and—
what was of still greater weight to Basil—he
had succeeded in introducing himself to Anthony Bidaud as the man he represented
himself to be. " There was an allusion to a
pretty niece." Then Chaytor was with
Annette, playing Basil's part. Was it likely
that Annette would be deceived ? Years had
passed since they had met, and the woman
might have reason to doubt her childhood's
memories. A cunning plausible villain this
Newman Chaytor. Successful in imposing
upon Annette, in wooing and perhaps win-

28*

ning her—Basil groaned at the thought—
what a future was before her! There was a
clear duty before him. To go to England
with as little delay as possible, and unmask
the plot.

That night he counted the money he had
saved; it amounted to two hundred and
thirty pounds. He could land in the old
country with a hundred and fifty pounds.
He consulted the exchange newspapers sent
to the office. In seventeen days a steamer
would start from Sydney for England. By
that vessel he would take his departure.

CHAPTER XI.

THE next morning Basil said to the editor, "I fear I am about to inflict a disappointment upon you."

"Wants a rise of salary," thought the editor. "All right; he shall have it." Aloud he said, "Go ahead."

"I wish you to release me from a promise."

"What promise?"

"When we made the engagement it was understood that I should not leave you without a month's notice."

"That was so," said the editor drily; and thought, "He's going to put the screw upon me that way. I am ready for him; I'll give him all he asks."

"I wish to leave without notice." The editor was silent, and Basil continued: "I am under great obligations to you; I have been very happy in your service, and I have done my best to please you."

"You have pleased me thoroughly; I hope I have said nothing to give you a different impression."

"Indeed you have not; no man could have acted fairer by me than you have done."

"Soft soap," thought the editor. "Have I been mistaken in him?" Aloud: "Well, then, I am sure you will act fairly by me. I cannot release you."

"You must; indeed you must. It is an imperative necessity."

"I can't see it. Look here. Are you going to start an opposition paper?"

"I have no intention of doing so. That would be a bad return."

"It would. Some other fellow, then, is going to start an opposition, and has made you a tempting offer."

"You are wrong. It is upon purely personal grounds that I shall have to leave. I am going home."

"Home! To England?"

"To England; and there is vital need of dispatch."

"Hallo!" thought the editor, "he has come into property. I knew he was highly connected." Aloud: "Now don't you be foolish. I am an older man than you, and therefore, on the face of it, a better judge of things. I don't expect a rise of salary would tempt you to remain."

" It would not."

" Not if I doubled what you are getting ? "

" Not if you were to multiply it by ten."

The editor considered before he spoke again. " Come, here's an offer for you. I will take you into partnership. You see the value I place upon your services. I'm dealing fair and square."

" You offer me more than I deserve, more than I accept. Nothing can tempt me to remain. I must leave Princetown ; I must leave the colony. I am called home suddenly and imperatively. You have been a good friend to me ; continue so, I beg, and release me at once. You talk of going home some day yourself. If all goes well with me we may meet in the old land and renew our friendship. You know me well enough, I trust, to be convinced that I would not desire to leave you so abruptly without some strong necessity. If you compel me to remain——"

" Oh ! you admit that I can compel you ? "

" The obligation is binding upon me, and

if you insist upon my giving you a month's notice it must be done, in honour. I cannot break my word."

"There speaks the gentleman," thought the editor, and gazed with admiration at the pleader.

"But you will be doing me," continued Basil, "an injury that may be irreparable. The delay may ruin my life, and the life of another very dear to me."

"I am a dunderhead," thought the editor. "There's a young lady mixed up in this." Aloud: "I should be sorry to do that; but you see the fix you place me in."

"It grieves me. I beg you to give me back my word."

"It comes so sudden. Why did you not tell me before?"

"Because I knew of nothing that called for my hasty departure until last night."

"There is something more than a business aspect of it. We have grown fond of you."

"I have grown fond of you and yours. I shall think of you with affection."

The editor was softened. "I will think it over, and let you know in the course of the day."

"It is only reasonable," said Basil, "that you should have time for consideration."

The subject was dropped. The editor consulted his wife, who was genuinely sorry at the prospect of losing Basil.

"I looked upon him as one of the family," she said, "and it will almost break Edith's heart to part with him." Then, with a woman's shrewd wit, she added, "Let us try what Edith can do to persuade him out of his resolution."

Away went Edith half an hour afterwards to seek Basil and argue with him. She found him in the churchyard, standing by the grave of the baby angel.

"Mother says you are going away," said the child.

"Yes, my dear," said Basil. "I am very, very sorry."

"Oh! how I shall miss you," said Edith, the tears springing to her eyes. "Won't you stay if I ask you?"

"I cannot, dear child. Dry your eyes. We shall meet again by-and-by."

She put her handkerchief to her eyes, but her tears flowed fast, and she sat by the grave and sobbed as if her heart was breaking.

"Listen to me, Edith," said Basil, sitting beside her and taking her hand. "If baby angel was a long, long way from here, and was in trouble and cried for you to come to her, would you not go to help her?"

"Yes, I would, I would; and they would take me to her."

"I am sure they would, for you have good parents, my dear. You told me when I first met you here that I had an angel, and that you were glad. Edith, my dear, my angel is calling to me to come and help her in her trouble. Would it not be very wrong for me to say, 'No, I will not come; I do not care for your trouble?'"

"It would be wicked."

"Yes, dear, it would be wicked, and I should not deserve your love if I acted so. When I first saw her she was a little girl like you; you reminded me of her, and I loved you because of that, and loved you better afterwards because of yourself. I shall always love you, Edith; I shall never, never forget you."

She threw her arms round his neck and lay in his embrace, sobbing more quietly.

"You can do something for me, Edith, that will fix you in my heart for ever."

"Can I? Tell me, and I will do it."

"Go to your father and say, 'You must let Basil go, father. His angel is calling for him, and it will be wicked if he does not go quickly.'"

"But that will be sending you away from me!"

"I know it will, my dear; but it will be doing what is right. If I remain I shall be very, very unhappy. You would not like me to be that?"

"No, no; I want you to be happy."

"Make me so, dear child, by doing as I bid you; and one day perhaps you will see my angel, and she shall love you as I do."

So by artfully affectionate paths he led her to his wish, and they went back hand in hand.

"Well," said the editor to Basil, later in the day, "you must have your way. The little plot we laid has failed, and Edith says you must go. You are a good fellow, and have served me well."

"I sincerely thank you. If I apply to you for a character you will give me one."

" Indeed I will; the best that man could
have. But there are conditions to my consent. You must stop till Thursday."

" I will do that."

" And you must act as ' Our Special Cor-
repondent ' at home. A letter once a month."

" I promise you."

" You have not beaten me entirely, you
see," said the editor good humouredly, " I
shall get something out of you. I am pleased
we shall part good friends."

They shook hands, and passed a pleasant
evening together.

The editor had a motive in stipulating that
Basil should remain till Thursday. He was
not going to let such a man leave Princetown
without some public recognition of his merits ;
and on the following day Basil received an
invitation to dine with the townsmen at the
principal hotel on the night before his departure. He gratefully accepted it ; he had
worked honestly, and had won his way into
the esteem of the inhabitants of the thriving
township.

It was a famous gathering, and there was
not room for all who . applied for tickets.
John Jones, of the Only Beehive, took the

chair. On his right sat Basil, on his left,
Mr. Majoribanks. The Government Camp
was worthily represented ; all the large storekeepers were present, and several of the
most prosperous miners. It was a gala
night ; the exterior of the hotel was gay
with flags of all nations, and the editor's
wife and Edith had stripped their garden of
flowers to decorate the table. The Governor
of the colony could scarcely have been more
honoured.

Of course there were speeches, and of
course they were reported in the *Princetown
Argus* the next morning. Basil's health was
proposed by John Jones in magniloquent
terms, which were cheered to the echo ; had
Basil's thoughts not been elsewhere, even in
the midst of this festivity, he would have
been greatly amused at the catalogue of
virtues with which he was credited by the
chairman, but as it was he could not help
being touched by the evident sincerity of the
compliments which were showered upon him.
Princetown, said John Jones, owed Basil a
debt which it could never repay. He had
elevated public taste, and had conferred
distinction upon the township by his rare

literary gifts. Great was their loss at his departure, but they had the gratification of believing that he would ever look back with affection upon the time he had spent in " our flourishing township." And they had the further gratification of knowing that they had a champion in the great world to which he was returning, and which he would adorn with his gifts. Before resuming his seat it was his proud task to give effect to one of the pleasantest incidents in this distinguished gathering. The moment it was known that Basil was about to leave them a movement was set afoot to present him with some token of their regard. In the name of the subscribers, whose names were duly set forth in the illuminated scroll which accompanied the testimonial, he begged to present to the guest of the evening, " a gold keyless lever watch, half-quarter repeater, dome half hunting case, three-quarter plate movement, best double roller escapement, compensated and adjusted, and with all the latest improvements." John Jones rolled out this elaborate description as though each item in it were a delicious morsel which could not be dwelt upon too long. Engraved upon the case was

a record of the presentation, which the
orator read amid cheers, and attached to the
watch was a gold chain, with another long
description, of which John Jones took care
not to miss a single word. Then came the
peroration, in which the chairman excelled
himself, its conclusion being, "I call upon
you now to drink, with three times three,
health and prosperity to our honoured guest,
a gentleman, scholar, and good fellow." He
led a hip, hip, hip, hurrah—hoorah—hoorah!
And a little one in (the giant of the lot),
"Hoo-o-o-o-rah-h-h-h!" Then they sang,
"For he's a jolly good fellow," in which
they were joined by all the gold-diggers at
the bar and in the High Street outside.
John Jones sat down beaming, and gazing
around with broad smiles, wiped his heated
forehead, and whispered to himself, "Bravo,
John Jones! Let them beat that if they
can!" The presentation of the watch and
chain was a surprise to Basil; the secret had
been well kept, and the generous-hearted
donors were rewarded by the short speech
which Basil made in response. It was
eloquent and full of feeling, and when he
had finished the cheers were renewed again

and again. The watch and chain were really a very handsome gift, and before Basil put them on they were passed round for general inspection. Then a sentimental song was sung, followed by another toast. (The story-teller must not omit to mention that the first proposed were loyal toasts, which were received with the greatest enthusiasm.) Other toasts and other songs followed, the health of everybody who was anybody being proposed and drunk with acclaim. One of the most effective speeches of the evening was made by the editor of the *Princetown Argus*, in response to the toast of " The Press." He paid full tribute to Basil, and said : " He is about to leave us, but we shall not lose him entirely. I take the greatest pride in announcing that he has accepted the post of special European correspondent to the *Princetown Argus*, and we shall look out eagerly for the polished periods in which he will describe the great events of the old world. We send a herald forth to represent us, and the mother country has reason to congratulate herself that our choice has fallen upon such a gentleman as our guest," &c., &c. It would occupy too many

pages to give a full report of the proceedings. Those who are curious in such matters
cannot do better than consult the columns of
the next morning's issue of the *Princetown
Argus*, in which the speeches were fully reported, with a complete list of the names of
those present on the notable occasion. The
party did not break up until the small hours,
and it is to be feared that some of the jolly
fellows, when they sang " Auld Lang Syne,"
were rather unsteady on their legs. Whether
the occasion furnished any excuse for this
sad lapse the present chronicler will not
venture to say. To judge from John Jones,
who was not the least of the offenders,
they were little the worse for it, for he
was attending to his Only Beehive, early
the following morning, as fresh as a lark.
But then John Jones was an exceptional
being.

The hardest parting was with Edith. The
child gave Basil a bunch of flowers and her
favourite doll. To refuse the doll would
have caused the little maid fresh sorrow, so
Basil accepted the token of affection, and
subsequently, before he left Sydney, sent
Edith another, with which she fell violently

in love, and christened it Basil, though it was of the female sex.

"Good-bye, my dear," said Basil, "and God bless you!"

Edith's voice was choked with tears, and she could only gaze mournfully at the friend who had supplied her with loving memories.

"Speed you well," said the editor; "hope we shall meet again."

"Good luck, mate!" was the farewell greeting of a number of friends; Basil did not know until now that he had so many. He waved his hand to them, and was gone. But he had not travelled two miles before he heard the sound of a horse's hoofs galloping after him. He turned and saw Mr. Majoribanks.

"It just occurred to me," said the Goldfields' Warden, "that the name of the money-lender I met in Paris, through whom I became acquainted with your namesake, might be useful."

"It is very thoughtful of you," said Basil, "it ought to have occurred to me."

"I know no more about him than I have already told you," said Mr. Majoribanks,

" and I am not acquainted with his address, but I believe he lives in London. His name real or assumed—for some of his fraternity trade under false names—is Edward Kettlewell."

" Thank you," said Basil; " I shall remember it.'

Mr. Majoribanks kept with him for another mile, and then galloped back to the township. The steamer in which Basil took his passage home started punctually to the hour, and bore Basil from the land in which he had met with so many sweet and bitter experiences; and on the forty-fifth day from that of his departure he set foot once more in England.

CHAPTER XII.

For cogent reasons Basil had travelled home
third-class. It economised his funds — of
which he felt the necessity—and it enabled
him the better to carry out his wish of not
making friends on board. The task upon
which he was engaged rendered it advisable
that as little curiosity as possible should be
aroused respecting himself and his personal
history. That he should have to work to
some extent in secresy was not congenial to
his nature, but by so doing he would have a
better chance of success. Until he came face
to face with Newman Chaytor it was as well
that his operations should be so conducted
as not to put his treacherous comrade on his
guard.

He had ample time on board ship to review
the events of the past few years, and although
he found himself wandering through laby-
rinths of extreme perplexity as to the doings

of Newman Chaytor, the conclusion was forced upon him that his false friend had practised towards him a systematic course of treachery and deceit. He had read accounts of men returning home from distant lands for the express purpose of personating others to whom they bore some close personal resemblance, and one famous case presented itself in which such a plot was only exposed by the wonderful skill of the agents employed to frustrate it. There, as in his own case, a large fortune hung upon the issue, but Newman Chaytor had been more successful than the impostor who had schemed to step into the enjoyment of a great estate. Chaytor had obtained possession of the fortune, and was now enjoying the fruits of his nefarious plot. But Basil's information was so imperfect that he was necessarily completely in the dark as to the precise means by which Newman Chaytor had brought his scheming to this successful stage. He knew nothing whatever of the correspondence which Chaytor had carried on with his uncle and Annette. Determined as he was to spare no efforts to unmask the villain, such a knowledge would have spurred him on with indignant fierceness. To recover his fortune, if it were possible to do so, was the lesser incentive; far more important was it, in his estimation, that Annette should be saved from the snare which had been prepared for her.

It was with strange sensations that he walked once more through familiar thoroughfares, and noted that nothing was changed but himself. Since last he trod them he had learnt some of life's saddest lessons; but hope, and faith, and love remained to keep his spirit young. It was no light matter that he had been awakened from the dull lethargy of life into which he had fallen in the earlier days of Princetown; that his faith in human nature had been restored; that he had won affection and esteem from strangers who even now, though the broad seas divided them, had none but kindly thoughts for him. Foul as was the plot of which he was the victim, he had cause to be deeply grateful.

He took lodgings on the Lambeth side of Westminster Bridge, two modest rooms, for which he paid seven shillings a week; food would cost him little; his modest resources must be carefully husbanded, and he would be contented with the humblest fare. His

task might take long in the accomplishment,
and to find himself stranded in the City of
Unrest would be fatal. His experiences had
been so far valuable that they assisted him to
a more comprehensive view of the circumstances of life. When he was last in England
he had thought little of the morrow. Now it
had to be reckoned with.

In considering how he should set about his
task, he had decided that it would be advisable to call in professional assistance. He
had not arrived at this decision without long
deliberation. He detested the means, but
repugnant as the course was to him he felt
that they were justifiable. Singularly enough
he had, without being aware .of it, taken
lodgings in a house, the master of which belonged to the class he intended to call to his
aid. He arrived at this knowledge on the
second day of his tenancy. Children always
attracted him, and his landlady had four, all
of them boys, with puffy cheeks and chubby
limbs. Their ages were three, five, seven,
and nine, a piece of information given to him
by their mother as he issued from the house
on the second morning, and stood by her side
a moment watching their antics. The word

is not exactly correct, for their pastime was singularly grave and composed. The eldest boy wielded a policeman's truncheon, and his three brothers, standing in a line, were obeying the word of command to march, a few steps this way, a few steps that, to halt, and finally to separate and take up positions in distant doorways, from which they looked severely at the passers-by.

"Bless their hearts!" said the proud mother. "They're playing policemen."

"They seem to know all about it," remarked Basil.

"They ought to," responded the mother. "It was born in them."

"Is your husband a policeman?" asked Basil.

"He was, sir," replied the mother; "but he has retired from the force, and belongs now to a private inquiry."

Basil thought of this as he walked away, after patting the children on the head, who did not know exactly whether to be gratified at the mark of attention, or to straightway take the stranger into custody. He had not seen his landlord yet, and it had happened, when he engaged the rooms from the woman, that, with the usual carelessness of persons in her station in life, she had not asked her new lodger's name, being perfectly satisfied of his respectability by his paying her a fortnight's rent in advance, and informing her that he would continue to do so as long as he remained in the house. Basil was afraid, if he went to a regularly established private office, that the fees demanded would be higher than his slender resources warranted, and bent as he was upon economising, he saw here a possible opportunity of obtaining the assistance he needed at a reduced rate. Therefore on the evening of this day he tapped at the door of the sitting-room, in which his landlord was playing a game of "old maid" with three of his children, and intimated his desire for a little chat with the man after the youngsters had gone to bed.

"On business," said Basil.

"No time like the present, sir," said the landlord, who saw "with half an eye," as he subsequently expressed himself, that his tenant was a gentleman; "I'll come up to your room at once, unless you prefer to talk here."

"We shall be more private up-stairs," said Basil, and up-stairs they went to discuss the business.

As a preliminary the landlord handed Basil a card, with "Mr. Philpott," printed on it, and in a corner, "Private Inquiry," to which was added the address of the house in which they were sitting.

"Do you carry on your business here, then?" inquired Basil.

"Partly, sir," replied Mr. Philpott. "I am engaged at an office in Surrey Street, but it is seldom that my time is fully occupied there, and as I am not on full pay I stipulate that I shall be free to undertake any little bit of business that may fall into my hands in a private way."

"That may suit me," said Basil. "To be frank with you, I was looking out for some one who would do what I want at a reasonable rate; I am not overburdened with funds, but I can afford to pay moderate fees. Will that meet your views?"

"Yes, sir. If you will tell me what you want done I will let you know about how much it will cost."

Basil paused before he commenced; he was

dealing with a stranger, and he did not wish to disclose his name.

" What passes between us is in confidence, Mr. Philpott ? "

" Altogether in confidence, sir. That is one of the rules of our profession. Whether anything comes of it or not, I shall say nothing of my client to a third party, unless you instruct me otherwise."

" You are sometimes consulted by people who desire to conceal their names? "

" Oh, yes, but they are not generally so frank as you are. You would rather not tell me your name ? "

" That is my desire, if it will make no difference."

" Not an atom of difference. Say Mr. Smith."

" I am obliged to you. I need not, then, disclose my own particular interest in the matter."

" Not at all, if it will not hamper me."

" I don't see how it will hamper you in the least. Shall I pay you a modest retainer ? Will a guinea do ? "

" A guinea will do, sir. Thank you."

" You had better take notes of what I say,

Mr. Philpott." The private inquiry agent produced his pocketbook. "Write down first the names I give you."

Mr. Philpott took down the names and addresses of Mr. Bartholomew Whittingham and of the lawyers in London who transacted that gentleman's affairs when Basil was last in England ; also the name of Mr. Basil Whittingham.

"Any address to this name, sir ? " asked Mr. Philpott.

"None. Mr. Bartholomew Whittingham is, or was—for I understand he is dead—a gentleman of considerable fortune ; Mr. Basil Whittingham is his nephew ; the lawyers whose names I have given you transacted the old gentleman's business for many years, but I am not aware whether they have continued to do so."

" That is easily ascertained."

" Mr. Bartholomew Whittingham had neither wife nor children, and some years since it was his intention to leave all his property to his nephew. The young man, however, offended his uncle, and the old gentleman thereupon informed his nephew that he had destroyed the will he had made in his favour, and that Mr. Basil Whittingham might consider himself disinherited. Do you understand it thus far?"

"It is perfectly clear, sir."

"The relations between the uncle and his nephew were completely broken off. Mr. Basil Whittingham—who had some private fortune of his own, but had got rid of it—being disappointed in his expectations, left England for Australia, where he resided for a considerable time."

"For how many years shall we say, sir?"

"Five or six. When he was near his end the uncle repented of his decision, and made another will—I am supposing that he really destroyed the first, which may or may not have been the case—by which his original intention was carried out, and his nephew was constituted sole heir to the property."

"Good."

"This property, I believe, was not in real estate, but in cash and securities which were easily convertible. The knowledge of his kindness reached the nephew's ears in Australia, and he returned home and took possession of the fortune."

"Very natural."

"I wish these details to be verified, or otherwise, Mr. Philpott."

"I undertake to do so, sir."

"I wish also to ascertain where Mr. Basil Whittingham is now residing."

"Can you give a clue, sir?"

"A very slight one, I am afraid. The last I heard of the nephew was that about eighteen months ago he was in Paris, in the company of a Mr. Edward Kettlewell, a money-lender, whose offices are, or were, in London. I am under the impression that Mr. Basil Whittingham and Mr. Kettlewell may have had some business transactions with each other. If so, it should not be difficult to trace Mr. Basil Whittingham through Mr. Kettlewell."

"It may be more difficult than you imagine," said Mr. Philpott. "These money-lenders are difficult persons to deal with. They are as jealous of their clients as a cat of her kittens. 'Hands off,' they cry; 'this is my bird.' Hold hard a minute, sir. I have this year's 'London Directory,' down stairs."

He left the room, and returned bearing the bulky volume, which he proceeded to consult. No Mr. Edward Kettlewell, money-lender or financial agent, was to be found in its pages. There were plenty of Kettlewells, and a few Edwards among them, but not one who dealt in money.

"Still," said Mr. Philpott, "it may be one of these. He may have retired, he may have left the country, he may be dead. I will look through the directories for a few years past, and we will see if we can find him."

"My information concerning him," said Basil, "is not very exact, and may after all be incorrect; but with or without his assistance it is most important that the address of Mr. Basil Whittingham should be ascertained."

"I will do my best, sir; no man can do more."

"There is another matter, of which I must beg you not to lose sight. Shortly after Mr. Basil Whittingham arrived in Australia he came in contact with a gentleman, M. Anthony Bidaud, who owned a plantation in Queensland. This gentleman had a daughter, quite a child then, whose name is Annette. M. Anthony Bidaud died suddenly, and left no will. On the morning of his death a brother and sister—the brother's name, Gilbert—

presented themselves at the plantation, and the brother administered the estate, and assumed the guardianship of his niece. The plantation was sold, and the little girl, with her uncle and aunt, came to Europe. Between the child and Mr. Basil Whittingham there existed a bond of affection, and since his return to England he has succeeded—so my information goes — in establishing friendly relations with M. Gilbert Bidaud. If you are fortunate enough to trace Mr. Basil Whittingham, my impression is that the knowledge will lead you straight to M. Gilbert Bidaud and his sister and niece, to discover whom I consider of far greater importance than the discovery of the young man. Now, Mr. Philpott, if you have grasped the situation, are you prepared to set to work ? "

" I will not lose a day, sir ; I commence my inquiries to-morrow ; and as you inform me that you are not exactly rich it may be convenient if I present a weekly account, including all charges to date, so that you may know how you stand as to expenses. Then you can go on or stop at your pleasure."

" It will be the best plan," said Basil.

Mr. Philpott was very much puzzled that night when he thought over the commission entrusted to him. "He says nothing of himself," thought the private inquiry agent, " nor of the particular interest he has in the matter. He must have a particular interest —a very particular interest, for I never saw any one more in earnest than he is. His voice absolutely trembled when he spoke of the uncle and Mdlle. Annette. Now that would not happen if he were acting as an agent for another person. What is the conclusion, then? That he is acting for himself. Dŏes this Mr. Basil Whittingham owe him money? Perhaps. And yet it does not strike me as an affair of that kind. Well, at all events, he has acted openly and straightforwardly with me so far as he and I are concerned. It is not often a client tells you that he is living under an assumed name. I must ask the wife if his shirts and handkerchiefs are marked."

His curiosity, however, was destined not to be appeased; his wife told him that Basil's clothing bore no initials—which, according to Mr. Philpott's way of thinking, betokened extreme caution, and whetted his curiosity. He did not, however, allow this to interfere with the zealous exercise of his duties. Proceeding step by step he presented his weekly reports to Basil. In the course of a short time Basil's worst suspicions were confirmed. Newman Chaytor had come home and representing himself to be Basil Whittingham, had experienced no difficulty in establishing his position and administering his uncle's estate. This done, he had disappeared, and Mr. Philpott was unsuccessful in tracing him.

"But," said Basil, " would not a man, arriving from a country so distant as Australia, in such circumstances have to prove his identity ? "

Mr. Philpott opened his eyes at this question ; to use his own term, he " smelt a rat."

" Certainly he would," replied Mr. Philpott, " But that was simple enough in Mr. Basil Whittingham's case. He had been in correspondence with his uncle for some time previous to his departure from Australia."

" What do you tell me ? " cried Basil.

" It is an established fact," said Mr. Philpott expressing no surprise ; but Basil's tone, no less than his words, opened his eyes still further. " A few days before Mr. Bartholomew Whittingham's death he wrote to his nephew in Australia, announcing his change of intention. This letter was forwarded to Mr. Basil by his uncle's lawyers, who, as you now know, are not the same he employed in former years."

"Basil Whittingham," said Basil, unable to repress his excitement, "received these letters in Australia?"

"Undoubtedly. He brought them home with him, and others also which he had previously received from his uncle's lawyer's."

"There was a regular correspondence with them, then?"

"Yes, extending over a considerable time."

This was a fresh and startling revelation to Basil. Newman Chaytor had not only personated him in England, but had personated him at a distance, receiving letters intended for him and forging letters in reply.

"He robbed me of my papers," groaned Basil inly, "and obtained possession of the means to prove him the man he represented himself to be. The base, unutterable villain! He smiled in my face, a living lie! And I trusted in him, believed in him, laid my heart bare to him, and all the time he was planning my destruction. Just Heaven! Give me the

30*

power to bring him to the punishment he deserves!"

But did the foul plot go farther than this? Every time Chaytor returned from the colonial post-office it was with the same answer —there were no letters for Basil Whittingham. And he had received and answered them; they were on his person while he was uttering the infamous falsehood, smiling in Basil's face the while. To what depths would human cunning and duplicity go? The tale, related to Basil by one who had been wronged, would have sounded incredible. He would have asked, "Is not this man labouring under some monstrous delusion?" But the bitter experience was his, and no tale would now be too wild for disbelief. Again he asked himself, did the plot go farther than what had already come to his knowledge? Newman Chaytor, going to the post-office for letters for him, would receive all addressed to his name.

What if Annette had written? It was more than possible, it was probable; it was more than probable, it was true. At this conclusion he quickly arrived. Annette had redeemed her promise; she had written to him as she said she would, and had received

Chaytor's letters in reply. This explained how it was that Chaytor had been able to find Annette and her uncle. Did Gilbert Bidaud suspect, and was he trading upon the suspicion; and were the two villains conspiring for the destruction of the poor girl's happiness? Basil looked around pitifully, despairingly, as though invoking the assistance of an unknown power.

"You seem disturbed," said Mr. Philpott, who had been attentively observing him.

"The news you have imparted," said Basil, "is terrible. Is there no way of discovering this Basil Whittingham?"

"We might advertise for him," suggested Mr. Philpott.

Basil shook his head. "If he saw the advertisement he would not answer it."

"Hallo," thought Mr. Philpott, "our absent friend has done something that would place him in the criminal dock." Professionally he was in the habit of hiding his hand, so far as the expression of original thought went. "But some one who knows him," he said, "might see the advertisement, and answer for him."

Basil caught at the suggestion. "Advertise, then, and in such a manner as not to alarm him."

"Trust me for that," said Mr. Philpott, with great confidence. "I know how to bait my line."

But the advertisements met with no response. Worked up to fever heat, Basil instructed Mr. Philpott to spare no expense, and the inquiry was prosecuted with wasted vigour, for at the end of two months they had not advanced a step. Basil was in agony; he grew morbid, and raised up accusing voices against himself. The reflection that Annette, the sweet and innocent child who had given him her heart, should be in the power of two such villains as Gilbert Bidaud and Newman Chaytor was an inexpressible torture to him. He had accepted from her father a sacred trust—how had he fulfilled it? He inflicted exquisite suffering upon himself by arguing that it was he who had betrayed her, that it was through him she had been brought to this pass. Had she not known him she would never have known Newman Chaytor; had he not worked upon her young affections and extracted her promise to write to him it would have been impossible that Chaytor

should ever have crossed her path. He
pressed into this self-condemnation all the
cruel logic his mind could devise. As he
walked the streets at night Annette's image
rose before him and gazed upon him reproachfully. "You have compassed my ruin," it
seemed to say, "you are the cause of my
corruption, of my dishonour." He accepted
the accusation, and groaned, "It is I, it is I,
who have made your life a waste!" Of all
the dolorous phases through which he had
passed this perhaps was the worst. But he
had yet other bitter experiences to encounter.
On a Saturday evening Mr. Philpott said:

"I must speak honestly. I have done all I
could, and nothing has come of it. I might
continue as long as you continued to engage
my services, but it would be only throwing
your money away."

It was an unusual confession for a man in
his line to make. Private inquiry agents
have generally the quality of the leech, and
will suck the last drop of blood out of a
client, but Basil had won the commiseration
of his landlord.

"I must take the case into my own hands,"
said Basil gloomily. "I intended, indeed, to

tell you as much myself — for pressing
reasons. I thank you for all you have done
for me."

"Little enough," said Mr. Philpott. "I
wish you better luck than I have had. Mind
you, I don't give it up entirely, but if I do
anything more it will not be for pay."

"You are, and have been, very kind.
Have you made out your account?"

Mr. Philpott presented it, and Basil settled
it. Then he said:

"Will you ask your wife to step up and see
me?"

"Yes, sir. Now don't you be cast down,
sir; it is a long lane that has no turning, and
there's no telling at any moment what may
turn up. I should like to take the liberty of
asking one question."

"Ask it."

"If, after all, the search should be successful, is it likely you would be in a better
position than you are now? I am taking a
liberty, I know, but I don't mean it as such.
You told me at first you were not overburdened with funds; if it has been all going
out and none coming in, you must be worse
off now."

" I am very much worse off, Mr. Philpott. I will answer your question. Should I succeed in finding the man I am hunting—a poor hunt it has proved to be, with no quarry in view—I have reason to believe that I should obtain funds which would enable me to discharge any liabilities I may incur."

" Thank you, sir," said Mr. Philpott, pushing across the table the money which Basil had paid him; " then suppose I wait."

" No," said Basil gently, " take it while you are sure of it, and you have a family."

" But I can afford to wait, sir. If I lost ten times as much it would not break me."

" I must insist upon your taking it, Mr. Philpott."

It was the pride of the poor gentleman, who would leave himself penniless rather than leave an obligation unsettled. Mr. Philpott recognised it as such, and recognised also that it marked the difference between them—which increased the respect he felt for Basil. He pocketed the money reluctantly.

" Send your wife up to me, Mr. Philpott."

" I will, sir."

Basil had indeed pressing reasons for dispensing with Mr. Philpott's further services.

The larger expenses of the last few weeks had brought his funds to a very low ebb. He took out his purse and counted his worldly wealth ; it amounted to less than two pounds. He was standing at poverty's door. In Australia, on the gold-fields, it would not have mattered so much. Earnest labour there can always ensure at least food for the passing day ; it is only the idle and dissolute and men without a backbone who have to endure hunger ; but here in this overcrowded city hunger is no rare experience to those who are willing to toil. Needless to say that the watch and chain which had been presented to Basil in Princetown was no longer in Basil's possession. The prospect before him, physically and morally, was appalling.

There was a gentle knock at the door. "Come in," said Basil, and Mrs. Philpott entered the room.

" My husband tells me you wish to see me, sir," said the landlady.

" Take a seat, Mrs. Philpott," said Basil. " I hope you have brought your weekly account; you should have given it to me yesterday."

"Friday's an unlucky day, sir," said Mrs. Philpott, fencing.

"But to-day is Saturday," said Basil with a sad smile.

"There's no hurry, sir, I assure you."

Basil looked at her and shook his head. His look, and the weary, mournful expression on his face, brought tears to the good creature's eyes.

"I must insist upon having the account, Mrs. Philpott.

"Well, sir, if you insist," said Mrs. Philpott, reduced to helplessness ; "it is only the rent, seven shillings."

"There are my breakfasts," said Basil, "with which you have been good enough to supply me. I have not kept faith with you. When I took these rooms I promised to pay always a fortnight's rent in advance ; lately I have not done so."

"How could you pay, sir, when you didn't know what the breakfasts came to ?"

"That does not excuse me. Oblige me by telling me how much I owe you."

"If you won't be denied, sir, it's twelve and tenpence.

"There it is, and I am infinitely obliged to

you.   Mrs. Philpott, I am sorry to say I must
give you a week's notice."

"You're never going to leave us, sir! Is
there anything wrong with the rooms? We'll
have it put right in a twinkling."

"The rooms are very comfortable, and I
wish I could remain in them ; but it cannot
be."

"You must remain, sir, really you must. I
won't take your notice. You *must* sleep
somewhere! Philpott will never forgive me
if I let you go."

Her consciousness of the strait he was in,
and her pity for it, were so unmistakable—her
desire to befriend him and her sympathy were
so clearly expressed—that Basil covered his
eyes with his hand, and remained silent awhile.
When he removed his hand he said :

"I am truly sensible of your goodness, Mrs.
Philpott, but it must be as I say."

"Think better of it, sir," urged Mrs.
Philpott. "You are a gentleman and I am
only a common woman, but I am old enough
to be your mother, and I don't think you
ought to treat me so—so"—exactly the
right word did not occur to her, so she added
—"suddenly. Here you are, sir, all alone, if

you'll excuse me for saying so, and here *we* are with more rooms in the house than we know what to do with. Why, sir, if you'll stay it will be obliging us."

All her kindly efforts were unavailing. She asked him to make the notice a month instead of a week, and then she came down to a fortnight, and made some reference to clouds with silver linings; but Basil was not to be prevailed upon, and she left the room in a despondent state.

" We'll keep an eye on him if we can," her husband said to her when she gave him an account of the interview. " I may find out something yet that will be of use to him. It is a strange case, old woman, and I don't mind confessing that I can't see the bottom of it."

CHAPTER XIII.

STERNLY resolved to carry out his determination not to occupy rooms for which he could not pay, Basil left Mrs. Philpott's house on the appointed day. It was his wish to quit without being observed, but Mrs. Philpott was on the look-out and lay in wait for him. Before he reached the street door she barred his way in the landing.

"You're not going away, sir," she said reproachfully, "without wishing the children good-bye."

In honest and affectionate friendship there is frequently displayed a pleasant quality of cunning which it does one no harm to meet with, and in her exercise of it Mrs. Philpott pressed her children into the service. Basil had no alternative but to accompany her into the parlour, where the four little fellows were sitting at the table waiting for dinner.

"You'll excuse me a minute, sir," said the

good woman; "if I don't fill their plates
before they're five minutes older they'll set
up a howl."

Out she bustled, and quickly returned with
a mighty dish of Irish stew.

"Philpott says," said Mrs. Philpott as she
placed the steaming dish on the table, "that
no one in the world can made an Irish stew
like mine; and what father says is law, isn't
it, children? I always have dinner with
them, sir; perhaps you'll join us. I really
should like to know if you're of my husband's opinion. Now this looks home-like."
—as Basil, who had independence of spirit,
but no false pride, took his seat at the table
where a chair and a plate had already been
set for him—"almost as if father was with
us, or as if the children had a great big
brother who had been abroad ever so many
years, and had popped in quite sudden to
surprise us."

All the time she was talking she was filling
up the plates, and the little party fell-to
with a will, Basil eating as heartily as the
rest. Mrs. Philpott was delighted at the
success of her ruse, but she was careful not
to show her pleasure, and when Basil said,

in answer to her inquiry, that he had had
enough, she did not press him to take more.
When dinner was over the children had to
be taken out of the room to have their faces
washed ; they were brought back for Basil
to kiss, and then were sent into the street to
play policemen.

"You'll let us hear of you from time to
time, sir," said Mrs. Philpott, as she and
Basil stood at the street door. " Philpott is
regular down-hearted because of your going.
I'm not to let your rooms again, he says, so
there they are, sir, ready for you whenever
you do us the pleasure to come. We're
getting along in the world, sir, and the few
shillings a-week don't matter to us now."

" I am truly glad to hear it, Mrs. Philpott,"
said Basil.

" There was a time," continued Mrs. Philpott, " when it did matter, and when every
shilling was worth its weight in gold in a
manner of speaking. We've had our ups
and downs, sir, as most people have, and if
it hadn't been for a friendly hand heaven
only knows where we should be at this
present minute. We were in such low water,
sir, we didn't know which way to turn.

Philpott says to me, 'Mother,' he says——
I hope I'm not wearying you, sir," said Mrs.
Philpott, breaking off in the middle of her
sentence.

"Pray go on," said Basil, feeling that it
would be churlish to check her.

"It's a comfort, sir," continued Mrs. Philpott, "to open one's heart. It doesn't make
me melancholy to look back to those days,
though my spirit was almost broke at the
time; I'm proud and grateful that we've
tided them over, with the help of God and
the good friend He sent us. 'Mother,' says
Philpott to me, 'I'm on my beam ends.
We're in a wood, and there's no way out
of it.' 'Don't you go on like that, father,'
I says; 'you keep on trying, and you'll
see a way out presently.' For I'm one of
that sort of women, sir, if you won't mind
my saying as much, who never give in and
don't know when they're beat. I don't mean
to say I don't suffer; I do, but I put a brave
face on it and never say die. 'You keep
on trying, father,' I says. 'Now haven't I
kept on trying?' says he. 'For eight weeks
I've answered every advertisement in the
paper, and applied for a job in hundreds and

hundreds of places without getting the smell
of one. I'm ashamed to look you in the face,
mother, for if it wasn't for you our boy would
starve.' We only had one then, sir, and as
for being ashamed to look me in the face
Philpott ought to have been ashamed to say
as much. All that I did was to get a day's
charing wherever I could, and a bit of washing when I heard there was a chance of it,
and that was how we kept the wolf from the
door. But I fell ill, sir, and couldn't stir out
of doors, and was so weak that I couldn't
stand at the wash-tub without fainting away.
Things were bad indeed then, and Philpott
took on so that I did lose heart a bit. Well,
sir, when we'd parted with everything we
could raise a penny upon, when we didn't
know where we should get our next meal
from, though it was only dry bread, heaven
sent us a friend. An old friend of Philpott's,
sir, that he hadn't seen for years, and that
he'd been fond of and kind to when he was a
young man, before he kept company with
me. Philpott had lent him a couple of pound,
and he'd gone off to America, and now, sir,
now, in the very nick of time, he came home
to pay it back. Did you ever see the sun

shine as bright as bright can be in a dark room at ten o'clock at night—for that was the time when Philpott's friend opened the door, and cried, ' Does Mr. Philpott live here ? ' It shone in our room, sir, though there was never a candle to light it up, and Philpott was sitting by me with his head in his hands. Philpott starts up in a fright— when people are in the state we were brought to the least unexpected thing makes their hearts beat with fear—he starts up and says, ' Who are you ? ' ' That's Philpott's voice,' says our friend. ' I'd know it among a thousand ; but don't you know mine, old fellow? And what are you sitting in the dark for ? ' Then he tells us who he is, and Philpott takes hold of his hand and says he's glad to see his old friend—which he couldn't, sir—and, ashamed of his poverty, pulls him out of the room. He comes back almost directly, and stoops over me and kisses me, and whispers that heaven has sent us a friend when most we needed one, and I feel my dear man's tears on my face. Then, sir, if you'll believe me, it seemed to me as if the sun was shining in our dark room, and all the trouble in my mind flew straight away.

31*

From that time all went well with us ; it was right about face in real earnest. Philpott's friend had another friend who got my husband in the force, and now we've got a bit of money put by for a rainy day, and don't need the rent for a couple of empty rooms."

Mrs. Philpott's account of her troubles was much longer than she intended to make it, and her concluding words were spoken wistfully and appealingly. They were not lost upon Basil, but they did not turn him from his purpose. With a kindly pressure of her hand, and promising to call and see her unless circumstances prevented—which meant unless his fortunes remained in their present desperate condition—he took his leave of her and passed out of her sight.

"Poor young gentleman," sighed the good woman. "I would have given the world if he'd have stopped with us. What on earth will become of him? It's hard to come down like that. Better to be born poor and remain so, than to be born rich and lose everything. His face was the image of despair, though he was politeness itself all the time I was talking. I sha'n't be able to get him out of my head."

She and her husband talked of him that
night, and if kind wishes and sympathising
words were of practical value, Basil would
have been comforted and strengthened.

Strengthened in some poor way he was.
It had been his hard fate to be made the
victim of as black treachery as one man ever
practised towards another ; but he had met
with kindness also at the hands of strangers.
He strove to extract consolation from that
reflection. Heaven knows he needed it, for
he was now to make acquaintance with
poverty in its grimmest aspect. He was
absolutely powerless. He had debated with
himself various courses which might be said
to be open to a man in his extremity, but he
saw no possible road to success in any one of
them. The most feasible was that he should
go to a capable lawyer and endeavour to
enlist his skill on his behalf. But what
lawyer would listen to a man who presented
himself with a tale so strange and without
the smallest means to pay for services rendered ? It would be a natural conclusion
that he was mad, or that he, being Newman
Chaytor, was adopting this desperate expedient to prove himself to be Basil Whit-

tingham. That he was a gentleman was
true ; he had the manners of one, but so
had many who were not gentlemen. Then
his appearance was against him ; he had no
other clothes than those he stood upright in,
and these were shabby and in bad repair.
Even if he had possessed assurance, it would
not have served him—nay, it would have
told against him, as proclaiming, " Here is
a plausible scoundrel, who seeks to deceive
us by swagger." He was truly in a helpless
plight.

The necessity of living was forced upon
him, and to live a man must have money to
purchase food. Recalling the efforts made
by Mr. Philpott in his days of distress, as
described by that man's good wife, he applied
for situations he saw advertised, but there
were a hundred applicants for every office,
and he ever arrived too late, or was pushed
aside, or was considered unsuitable. In
one of his applications he was very nearly
successful, but it came to a question of
character, and he had no reference except the
editor of the *Princetown Argus*, who was
fourteen thousand miles away. What wonder
that he was laughed at and dismissed ? Then

he thought that his experiences on the goldfields and his training as a journalist might
help him, and he wrote some sketches and
articles and sent them to magazines and newspapers. He heard nothing of them after they
were dropped into the editorial boxes. The
fault may have been his own, for he had no
heart to throw spirit into his effusions, but his
state was no less pitiable because of that.
He felt as if indeed he had for ever lost his
place in the world. By day he walked the
streets, and at night occupied a bed in the
commonest of London lodging-houses. •At
first he paid fourpence for his bed, but latterly
he could afford no more than twopence, and
presently he would not be able to afford even
that. It was a stipulation of his nightly
accommodation that he should turn out early
in the morning, and this he was willing
enough to do, for he had but little sleep, and
the beings he was compelled to herd with
filled him with dismay. It was not their
poverty that shocked him; it was their language, their sentiments, their expressions of
pleasure in all that was depraved. He had
had no idea of the existence of such classes,
and now that he came face to face with them

he shrank from them in horror. Had they been merely thieves it is possible that he might have tolerated them, and even entertained pity for them, arguing that they were born to theft, that their parents had been thieves before them and had taught them no better; or that they had been driven into the ranks by sheer necessity; but it was the corruption of their souls that terrified him; it was the consciousness that with vice and virtue placed for them to choose, with means for each, they would have chosen vice and revelled in it. Amid all this corruption and degradation he maintained a pitiable self-respect and kept his soul pure. Often did he go without a meal, but he would listen to no temptations, electing by instinct, rather to suffer physically than to lower his moral nature to the level of those by whom he was surrounded. When he walked the streets by day he did not walk aimlessly and without purpose. It was probable enough that Newman Chaytor was in London, and if so the fortune of which he had obtained fraudulent possession would enable him to live in the best and most fashionable quarters of the city. Basil haunted those better localities,

and watched for the villain who had betrayed
him in the vicinity of the grand hotels, the
clubs, and the resorts of fashion in the parks.
Sometimes at night he lingered about the
high-class theatres to see the audience come
out. In the event of his meeting his enemy
he had no settled plan except that he would
endeavour to find out where he lived, and
through that knowledge to obtain access to
Annette.

One night he met with a strange adventure.
He had come from Covent Garden, where,
mingling in the crowd, he had watched the
audience issue from the Opera House, in
which a famous songstress had been singing.
It was an animated, bustling scene, but it was
impossible for a man in such sore distress to
take pleasure in it; neither did he draw
bitterness from the gaiety; he merely looked
on with a pathos in his eyes which was now
their usual expression. Frequently, in his
days of prosperity, had he attended the opera,
as one of the fashion, and heard this same
songstress, whose praise was on every man's
lips; now he was an outcast, hungry, almost
in rags, without even a name which the world
would accept as his by right of birth and

inheritance. It was a cold night, but dry—
that was a comfort to a poorly clad man.
Indeed, there is in all conditions of life something to be grateful for, if we would only seek
for it.

A curious fancy entertained Basil's mind.
He heard the carriages called out—"Lady
This's carriage," "Lord That's carriage."
"the Honourable T'other's carriage." How if
"Mr. Basil Whittingham's carriage" was called
out? So completely was he for the moment
lost to the sad realities of his position, so
thoroughly did the fancy take possession of
him, that he actually listened for the
announcement, and had it been made it is
probable that he would have pushed his way
through the crowd with the intention of
entering the carriage. But nothing of the
kind occurred. Gradually the theatre was
emptied, and the audience wended homeward, riding or a-foot, north, south, east, and
west, till only the fringe was left—night-birds
who filtered slowly to their several haunts,
not all of which could boast of roof and
bed. A nightbird himself, Basil walked
slowly on towards Westminster. He had
fivepence in his pocket, and no prospect of

adding anything to it to-morrow, and he was
considering whether he should spend twopence for a bed, or pass the night on a bench
on the Embankment. It was a weighty
matter to decide, as important to him as the
debate which was proceeding in the House,
upon which a nation's destiny hung. In
Parliament Street a young couple brushed
past him; they had been supping after the
theatre, and Basil heard the man address the
woman as "Little Wifey," and saw her nestle
closer to her husband's arm as he uttered this
term of endearment. For a moment Basil
forgot his own misery, and a bright smile
came to his lips; but it faded instantly, and
he trudged wearily on discussing the momen-
tous question of bed or bench. Undecided,
he found himself on Westminster Bridge,
where he stood gazing upon the long
panorama of lights from lamps and stars.
Were this wonderful and suggestive picture
situated in a foreign country, English people
would include it in their touring jaunts and
come home and rave about it, but as it is
situated in London its beauties are unheeded.

Basil, leaning over the stone rampart, looking down into the river, was presently con-

scious that some person was standing by his side. He turned his head, and saw a woman, who gazed with singular intentness upon him. She was neither young nor fair, but she had traces of beauty in her face which betokened that in her springtime she could not have been without admirers. Her age was about thirty, and she was well dressed. So much Basil took in at a glance, and then he averted his eyes and resumed his walk across the bridge. The woman followed him closely, and when he paused and gently waved her off, she said :

"Why do you avoid me? I want nothing of you."

"Good-night, then," said Basil in a kind voice, and would have proceeded on his way if the woman had not prevented him.

"No, not good-night, yet," she said. "Did you not understand me when I said I want nothing of you? It is true ; but happening to catch sight of your face as I was crossing the bridge I could not pass without speaking to you. It would have brought a punishment upon me—knowing what I know."

Being compelled by her persistence to a closer observance of her, Basil was moved to

a certain pity for her. There were tears in
her eyes and a pathos in her voice which
touched him. Desolate outcast as he was,
whom the world, if he proclaimed himself,
would declare to be an impostor, what kind
of manhood was that which would refuse a
word of compassion to a woman who appeared to be in affliction? His pitying
glance strangely affected her; she clung to the
stone wall and burst into a passion of tears.

"I am sorry for your trouble," said Basil,
waiting till she had recovered herself. "Can
I do anything to help you?"

"Nothing," she replied. "No one can
help me. I have lost all I loved in the world.
This is a strange meeting; I have been thinking of you to-day, but never dreamt I should
see you to-night. To-night of all nights!"

"Thinking of me!" exclaimed Basil in
amazement.

"You will not consider it strange," said
the woman, "when you know all. I could
not stop at home; I have been sitting by her
side since three o'clock, and then a voice
whispered to me, 'Go out for an hour, look
up to heaven where the Supreme Guide is,
and pray for a miracle.' So I came out, and

have been praying to Him to give her back to me."

"Poor woman!" murmured Basil, for now he knew from her words that she had lost one who was dear to her. "I pity you from my heart."

"You are changed," said the woman; "not in face, for I should have known you anywhere, but in your voice and manner. It is gentler, kinder than it used to be."

Basil did not answer her; he thought that grief had affected her mind, and that her words bore no direct relation to himself. He had no suspicion of the truth which was subsequently to be revealed to him.

"It is many years since we met," she said. "Have you been long in England?"

"A few months," said Basil.

"You have not made your fortune?"

"No, indeed."

"You look poor enough. Have you no money?"

"None," said Basil; and added hastily, "or very little."

"You have been unfortunate since your return home?"

"Very unfortunate."

She opened her purse, and took out a sovereign and held it out to him.

"Thank you, no," said Basil, his wonder growing.

" You are changed indeed," said the woman, " to refuse money. It is honestly come by. Two years ago I was married, and my husband, who died a year afterwards, left me a small income. It was more than I deserved, for I deceived him by telling him I was a widow. It made no difference, but still it was a deceit. Will you not take it?"

" No."

" And yet you need it?"

" Do not urge me further. Good night."

" Wait one moment. I was going to tell you to-night; but you had best see for yourself. It is your right. Here is my address; my mother and sister live with me. Come and see me to-morrow morning at ten o'clock. Promise me."

" No, I cannot promise," said Basil, moving away.

" You must promise," said the woman, moving after him. " I will not leave you till you do. I tell you it is your right—it is more than your right, it is your duty."

Seeing that there was no other way to release himself from her, Basil said, "I promise."

"On your sacred word of honour," said the woman.

"On my sacred word of honour."

"I will trust you; there was a time when I would not. Good night. To-morrow, at ten."

She glided away, and Basil was once more alone. The misery of his own circumstances was no encouragement to him to dwell upon the adventure, and he dismissed it from his mind, accounting for the woman's strange utterances by the supposition that she was of weak intellect. He passed the night in the open air, and in the morning bought one pennyworth of bread—it was cheaper than buying a penny roll—for his breakfast. This and water from a drinking-fountain satisfied hunger and thirst.

"A man can live upon very little," he said to himself, "but how is it going to end?"

It was a pertinent question, and answered itself. The end seemed near and certain.

It was a bright morning, and he walked in the sun. He did not forget the promise he had made to the woman; it was a promise to which he had pledged himself, and even if mischief resulted it must be fulfilled. The name on the card was Mrs. Addison, the address, Queen Street, Long Acre. Thither he went, and paused before a milliner's shop, the windows of which were partially masked by shutters. Over the shop front was the name Addison, and the goods displayed bore evidence of a certain prosperity; they were not of the poorest kind. An elderly, grey-haired woman came forward as he entered. Her face was sad and severe, and there was no civility in her voice as she informed him in answer to his question, that he had come to the right address.

"Go through that door," she said, with a frown, "up-stairs to the first landing. My daughter expects you. I must ask you to make your visit short."

It was not only that her voice was cold, it expressed repugnance, and without requesting an explanation Basil followed her and mounted the stairs. The sound of his footsteps brought the woman he had met on Westminster Bridge to the door of the front room.

"You have kept your promise," she said. "Come in."

A younger woman than she rose as he entered, cast one brief glance at him, and immediately left the room. The window blinds were down and the gas was lighted. His strange acquaintance of the previous night was dressed in deep mourning. Her face was white, and swollen with weeping.

"I prayed for a miracle last night," she said, "but my prayers were not answered. I had almost repented that I asked you to come, but still it is right, it is right. If you have a heart it should be a punishment to you for all you have made me suffer."

"I do not in the least understand you," said Basil.

Had it not been for her grief her look would have been scornful. She paid no heed to his words, but continued:

"When I said last night that I wanted nothing of you I said what I meant. When you go from here I wish never to see your face again. It will be useless for you to trouble me."

"I shall not trouble you," said Basil in a gentle tone, which seemed to make her waver ; but she would not yield to this softer mood.

"That you are poor to-day," she said, "and I am well-to-do, so far as money goes, proves that there is a Providence. Years ago —very soon after your desertion of me—I cast you from my·heart, and resolved never to admit you into it again. It might have been otherwise had you behaved honestly to me, for I loved you, and you made me believe that you loved me. It was better for me that the]tie which bound us should be broken. I have led a respectable life, and shall continue to do so. I am the happier for it."

"For heaven's sake," cried Basil, "explain what it is you accuse me of."

"Ask your own heart. Although there is an apparent change in you, you are still the same, I see, in cunning and duplicity. But I will listen to no subterfuges ; there is no possibility of your justifying yourself, and your power over me is gone. Towards you my heart is cold as stone."

"You are labouring under some singular delusion," said Basil, "and I can but listen to you in wonder."

"Still the same, still the same," said the woman. " You used to boast of your superior powers, and that you were so perfect an actor that you could make the cleverest believe that black was white. See what it has brought you to "—she pointed to his rags. " I have no pity for you ; as you have sown, so have you reaped. So might I have reaped had I not seen the pit you treacherously dug for me ; so might I have reaped had I not repented before it was entirely too late. I owe you this much gratitude—that it was your base desertion of me that showed me my sin. Had you remained I might have sunk lower and lower till grace and redemption were lost to me for ever. What expiation was possible for me I have made, with sincere repentance, with sincere sorrow for my error. It would be well for you if you could say the same. Yow saw my mother down-stairs. She cast me off, as you know, but she opened her arms to me when I convinced her of my sincerity, when I vowed to her on my knees to live a pure life. I am again her daughter. You see these drawn blinds, you see my dress, you see that this is a house of mourning. Can you guess what for? "

"Indeed I cannot," said Basil, "except that you have lost one who is dear to you. What comfort can I, a stranger, offer you that you cannot find for yourself? It is small consolation to say that your loss is a common human experience. Be faith your solace. There is a hereafter."

Her scorn and horror of him, now plainly expressed in her face, so overpowered her that she allowed him to finish without interruption.

"You, a stranger to me!" she cried. "Will you still wear the mask—or is it, *is* it possible that the rank selfishness and callousness of your nature can have made you forget? All was over between us—but a link remained, a link of sweet and beautiful love which the good Lord has taken from me. I bow my head; I will not, I must not rebel!" She folded her hands, and, moving to the darkened window, stood for a few moments there engaged in silent prayer. Presently she spoke again. "My fond hopes pictured a bright and happy future for her. I, her mother, would be for ever by her side, guiding her from the pitfalls which lay before young and confiding innocence. Her life should be without stain, without reproach. She did not know, she would never have known the stain which rests upon mine. It is revealed to her now. Forgive me, my darling, and look down with pity upon me! Yes, out of my sin I created a garden of love —for her, who was to me what sight would be to the blind, through whose sweet and pure influence I was led to the Divine throne. My fond hopes have been dashed to the ground—they are dead, never to be revived. Come with me."

With noiseless footsteps she walked out of the room, and Basil followed her to another on the same landing. Softly, tenderly, as though fearful of disturbing what was therein, she turned the handle, and she and Basil stood in the presence of death.

Of death in its fairest form. Upon the bed lay the body of a young girl whose age might be ten. The sweet beauty, the peace, the perfect rest in the child's face, moved Basil to tears; she looked like a sleeping angel.

"Oh, my darling, my darling!" sobbed the bereaved mother, sinking to her knees. "Pray for me; intercede for me. Unconsciously I strayed; I saw not my sin. Oh, child of shame and love, bring peace to my breaking heart, and do not turn from me when we meet above!"

Basil spoke no word; some consciousness of the truth was slowly coming to him. There was a silence in the room for several minutes; then the woman rose to her feet.

"Kiss her," she said. "When you last saw her she was a baby. If she were living, and saw your face, she would look upon you as a stranger; but now she knows the truth."

Then Basil understood. "Yes," he said inly, "now she knows the truth."

He stooped and kissed the child's lips, and the mother's tears broke out afresh; checking them presently, she said:

"It was by the strangest chance I met you last night. I have done what I conceived to be my duty. Now go," and she pointed to the door.

"I will obey you," said Basil; "but I must say a word to you first, in the next room."

She looked at him for a moment hesitatingly, then nodded her head, and they left the chamber of death as noiselessly as they had entered it.

"I did not intend it," said the woman, and taking a tress of fair hair from her bosom, and dividing it, she offered him a portion. "You may like to keep it as a remembrance."

"I thank you humbly," said Basil; "it may help me on my way."

A look of incredulous wonder flashed into her face, but remained there only an instant, and she shook her head as though she were answering a question she had asked mutely of herself.

"Before us lies an open grave," she said. "You and I speak now together for the last time on earth. I forgive you, as I hope to be forgiven. You have something to say to me?"

"Yes; and I entreat you, however strange you may think my question, to suspend your indignation for awhile, and answer me in plain words."

"I will endeavour to do so, if it is such a question as you should address to me."

"I will not fret you by arguments or expostulations. You have suffered deeply, and from my heart I pity you. Plainly, whom do you take me for?"

"For yourself—for no other man, be sure."

"But let me hear my name from your lips."

"As you insist upon it," she said, with sad contempt, "though such a farce should not be played at such a time; but when were you otherwise than you are? You are Newman Chaytor."

"I," said Basil, speaking very slowly, "am Newman Chaytor?"

"You are he; there lives not such another, and remembering all that has passed between us, remembering your vows and oaths, for that I say, thank God! If you have any reason for going by another name, for wishing to be known by another name—and you may have, heaven help you!—be sure that I will not betray you. You are dead to me, as I am dead to you."

"Look at me well," said Basil. "If you were upon your oath would you swear that I am the man you say I am?"

"To swear otherwise would be to swear falsely. What crime have you committed that you should stand in dread of being known?"

"None. It is not to be expected that you will believe when I tell you that you are the victim of delusion, as I am the victim of a foul and monstrous plot."

"Who would believe you? Denial is easy enough, and of course you will deny, having reason to do so. But come into the light."

She raised the blind, and he stepped to the window where the light shone upon his face.

"You are Newman Chaytor," she repeated, letting the blind fall.

He bowed his head, and said, "You have just cause for your pitiless resentment; and whether I am or am not the man you believe me to be, I bow my head before you in sorrow and shame. The day may come—I do not know how, or in what way it may be brought about, for I am at the extremity of misery—when, showing you this"—he touched his breast, where he placed the lock of her child's hair—"and recalling this interview, you will see the error into which you have innocently fallen. Till then, or for ever, farewell."

"One moment," said the woman, with trembling accents, "what has passed cannot be recalled, nor will I speak of the folly of your denial of the solemn truth. It is a meaningless proceeding."

"To me," said Basil, interrupting her, "it means everything. Honour, truth, fidelity, faith in virtue and goodness, all are at stake. It may never come to an issue, for the end seems near, but heaven may yet have some mercy in store for me. As you prayed for a miracle last night which was not vouchsafed you, so will I pray for a miracle to help me to a just conclusion of my bitter trials." A pitiful smile accompanied his words. "It is not for me, one suffering man among millions happier, I trust, than myself, to doubt Divine Goodness. The eternal principle of Justice remains, and will, now or hereafter, assert itself, as it has ever done. May peace, and comfort, and happiness be yours."

"I offered you money last night," said the woman, impressed by what he said, but making no comment upon it. "Will you not accept it now?"

"I thank you—no," he said, bowing to her with humility. "Farewell."

END OF VOL. II.

PRINTED BY
KELLY AND CO., GATE STREET, LINCOLN'S INN FIELDS,
AND MIDDLE MILL, KINGSTON-ON-THAMES.

www.ingramcontent.com/pod-product-compliance
Lightning Source LLC
Chambersburg PA
CBHW031343020726
47499CB00005B/1378